ANTHONY HOPE

The Prisoner of Zenda

古堡藏龍

Adaptation and activities by Elizabeth Ferretti
Illustrated by Barbara Baldi Bargiggia

The Commercial Press

Contents 目錄

故事錄音開始和結束的標記
start ▶ stop ◼

MAIN CHARACTERS

Princess Flavia

Rudolf Rassendyll

Black Michael
(Duke of Strelsau)

King Rudolf V
of Ruritania

Detchard

Antoinette
de Mauban

Fritz Von
Tarlenheim

Colonel Sapt

Reading and Speaking

1a *The Prisoner of Zenda* **is an exciting adventure story. It's set in the small European kingdom of Ruritania in the 1870s. Read this leaflet from the Ruritanian Tourist Office, then answer True or False below.**

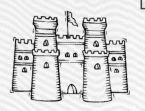

Come to Ruritania!

Our beautiful little country is situated to the south of Germany, and is easily reached by train from Dresden. There's something to interest everyone! Explore our forests, magical castles, and the lovely old town of Zenda. The capital, Strelsau, is a city of contrasts! From the station, you will walk down wide, modern streets, towards the historic heart of this great city. Don't miss a visit to our magnificent cathedral, and the palaces of the Ruritanian royal family.

	T	F
1 Ruritania is near Denmark.	☐	☐
2 Large areas of Ruritania are covered with trees.	☐	☐
3 Ruritania has a lot of beautiful old buildings.	☐	☐
4 Zenda is a historic town in Ruritania.	☐	☐
5 The capital city, Strelsau, is partly modern, with an old centre.	☐	☐
6 Ruritania is a republic.	☐	☐

1b Discuss the following in pairs

- Would you like to visit Ruritania?
- If you went there, what would you like to do?

Family and Relationships

2a **Read the following paragraph. Use a dictionary to check any words you don't know.**

My name is Rudolf Rassendyll and I'm the hero of this story. I'm the second son of an important English family, with plenty of money! My brother, Robert, is married to a lady called Rose. The Rassendylls usually have dark hair and dark eyes, but I don't. Once in a generation, someone in our family is born with red hair and a large nose, like me. This is because Lady Amelia Rassendyll, who lived 150 years ago, fell in love with a foreign prince, but... you will have to read Chapter 1 to find out what happened next!

2b **Use the phrases in the box below, to describe some characters in this story.**

> dark hair and eyes • fell in love • hero of the story • red hair and a big nose • Rudolf's sister-in-law • Rudolf's older brother • member of Rudolf's family from the past

1 Rudolf _____

2 Rose _____

3 Robert _____

4 Lady Amelia Rassendyll _____

Listening

3 **Read the sentences below. Now listen to the first part of Chapter 1, and write down the name of the person who said each one.**

1 'You've done nothing with your life except enjoy yourself!'

_____

2 'Why should I do anything?'

_____

3 'What *is* the matter with you two?'

_____

4 'His hair isn't his fault.'

_____

5 'Well, I like the red hair *and* the nose.'

_____

I Meet a King

▶ 2 'Rudolf Rassendyll, when in the world are you going to *do* something?' asked my sister-in-law, one day at breakfast. 'You are twenty-nine years old,' she continued, 'and you've done nothing with your life but enjoy yourself.'

I put my egg spoon down. 'My dear Rose,' I answered, 'why in the world should I do anything? I have *almost* enough money to do what I want – no one ever has *quite* enough money, you know – I come from an important and wealthy family. Your husband, my brother Robert, is Lord Burlesdon. That's enough for me.'

'Good families are generally worse than others,' she said, annoyed. Then she looked at my hair and said, 'I'm so glad that Robert's hair is black!'

At that moment, my brother walked in. 'What *is* the matter with you two?' he asked.

'She's complaining about me doing nothing, and having red hair,' I said, sounding hurt.

'His hair isn't his fault,' admitted Rose.

'It usually appears once in a generation,' said my brother, 'and the nose too, of course.'

'Well, I like the red hair *and* the nose,' I said, looking proudly at the portrait of my ancestor, Lady Amelia Rassendyll, that was hanging on the wall.

'I wish you'd take that picture away, Robert,' said Rose.
I laughed and continued with my breakfast.

❖ ❖ ❖

I always find explanations in stories boring, but now that I'm writing my own story, I find I need to include one here. My dear sister-in-law was embarrassed by my red hair and my large nose because of a scandal that happened in my family in 1733. At that time, young Prince Rudolf Elphberg of Ruritania came to visit King George II. Prince Rudolf stayed in England for several months, but left suddenly and mysteriously. During his visit he met my ancestor, Lady Amelia. Two months after Rudolf left, she gave birth to a son. Soon after that, Rudolf Elphberg became King Rudolf III of Ruritania.

If you walk through my brother's house, you'll see fifty family portraits from the last 150 years. Five or six of my ancestors have red hair, long, straight noses and blue eyes. All the other Rassendylls have dark hair and eyes.

That is the explanation, and I am glad to have finished it. This type of scandal can ruin a family. My sister-in-law disliked my Elphberg hair and nose because they reminded her of my family's bad character! But I can hardly be blamed for what Lady Amelia did, and in fact, I'd done more with my life than Rose thought. I'd been to a German school and university, and spoke German as well as I spoke English. I could speak French, a little Spanish and Italian. I could use a sword and gun well, could ride any horse, and keep a cool head in any situation. If I have nothing to do, you can blame my parents for leaving me so much money that I don't have to work.

'Well, I just want you to *do* something, Rudolf,' Rose said.

Rose looked so pretty, and she made me feel so guilty, how could I say no? I promised her that if I was still free in six months' time, then I would look for a job.

'Oh Rudolf,' she cried, 'how good of you. I *am* glad!'

❖ ❖ ❖

I now had six months of freedom. I loved travelling, so I decided to go and visit Ruritania. You may be surprised to learn that I'd never been to Ruritania. My father had always been secretly proud of our connection with the country's royal family (after all, he had called me Rudolf), but he'd always stopped me from going there. He was worried that I might have problems if I went because people would think I was an Elphberg. My brother agreed with him.

A few days later I read an article in *The Times* newspaper. There was a new King in Ruritania and his coronation[1] would be in three weeks' time. There would be a wonderful celebration in Strelsau, the capital city, to welcome the new King. I was determined to be there and I did not want anyone to stop me, so I kept my journey a secret. I told my family I was going to have a holiday in the Austrian mountains.

I arrived in Paris and booked in at The Continental. I called on my old friend, George Featherly, who works as a diplomat for the British Ambassador in Paris. We had dinner together in a fine restaurant, went to the opera, and then went to see the famous poet, Bertram Bertrand.

There were lots of people at Bertram's flat, but he looked terribly unhappy. At the end of the evening, I asked George what was worrying him. He laughed unkindly, and told me Bertram was in love with a well-known member of Paris society, Antoinette de Mauban. 'Bertram's problem is that she's fallen in love with someone else,' said George.

1. coronation: 加冕典禮

'I met him last month, a charming man, Prince Michael, Duke of Strelsau. He's the younger brother of the new King of Ruritania.

'The Duke's gone back to Strelsau now, to be at his brother's coronation,' continued George, 'He won't enjoy that very much though! He was the old King's favourite, you see, and I think he's disappointed not to be the next King of Ruritania. I also think Madame de Mauban will be disappointed. I hear that Michael's got his eye on someone else.'

The next day George went with me to the station, where I bought a ticket to Dresden.

'What are you doing in Dresden?' asked George. George was always gossiping[1]. If I'd told him I was going to Ruritania, then the news would have arrived in London in three days, and after less than a week my sister-in-law and brother would have heard of it! I was just thinking of something to say, when, fortunately, his attention was caught by someone else, and he rushed off. I watched where he was going, and saw him raise his hat to an attractive and fashionably dressed woman.

'Well, aren't you lucky?' George said, when he came back, 'That's Antoinette de Mauban, and she's going to Dresden too! It's rather strange though, because she doesn't want to meet you at the moment.'

I felt quite offended at that.

I spent the night in Dresden, and the next morning, Antoinette de Mauban got on the same train as me, though I didn't speak to her.

❖ ❖ ❖

When we got to the border with Ruritania, the police officer took my passport and then stared at me very rudely. I found out that Strelsau was full of people who'd come for the coronation, and I would have problems finding a room in a hotel. I decided to get out at a town called Zenda,

---

1. gossiping: 説三道四

which was 50 kilometres from the capital, and spend the night there.

I was given a warm welcome at the hotel in Zenda. It was owned by an old lady and her daughter, but I was surprised to find they were not at all interested in the coronation. The old lady liked Duke Michael better than the new King. 'Everyone knows Duke Michael,' she said, 'He owns the Castle of Zenda, and he's always lived here, but his brother Rudolf is almost a stranger. He's spent so much time abroad, that most of us don't even know what he looks like!'

Her daughter told me the King was staying in the forest near the hotel, as a guest of his brother.

'Are Michael and his brother friends, then?' I asked.

'They love each other as men do who want the same thing and the same wife!' said the daughter. 'Black Michael, I mean Duke Michael,' she said, looking over at her mother, 'would give his soul to marry his cousin, Princess Flavia, but everyone thinks she'll marry the King.'

At that point, a man called Johann came in. He stared at me and I thought he was very rude! The next day though, Johann was extremely kind and helpful. He told me he worked for the Duke at the Castle of Zenda, and said I could stay at his sister's house in Strelsau. I had several hours before my train left for Strelsau, so I sent my bags to the station, and set off to explore.

I walked up the steep hill above the town of Zenda to the castle and only half an hour later was standing in front of it. The castle was divided into two parts – an old part, surrounded by a wide, deep moat[1], and next to that, a more modern, comfortable castle. The only way into and out of the old castle was across a drawbridge[2] which could be opened and shut.

Well, I thought, walking on, if "Black" Michael can't be King or marry Princess Flavia, then at least he has a comfortable castle to live in!

---

1. **moat:** 護城河   2. **drawbridge:** 吊橋

❖ ❖ ❖

I went into the forest and walked for an hour. The place was beautiful, and it was cool under the trees. I found somewhere to sit and, leaning back against a tree, fell asleep.

When I woke, two men were standing in front of me, staring at me with great curiosity. They were both wearing hunting clothes and had guns. One was short and fat, with small, pale-blue eyes. The second was much younger and thinner, with dark hair.

'He's the same height, too,' the old man said, as I stood up. Then he came over to me, telling the younger man to follow. He raised his hat and greeted me politely. Then the young man also stepped forward and smiled.

'This,' he said, pointing to the older man, 'is Colonel Sapt, and I am Fritz von Tarlenheim. We're both in the service of the King of Ruritania.'

'My name is Rudolf Rassendyll. I've travelled from England to come to the coronation of your new King. I was in the service of the Queen of England, for a year or two,' I said.

'Then we are all brothers of the sword.' Fritz von Tarlenheim held out his hand and shook mine warmly.

'Rassendyll, Rassendyll,' muttered[1] Colonel Sapt, and then he remembered. 'I know who you are!' he said, excitedly, 'You're from the family of Lord Burlesdon. I knew it from the colour of your hair. You know that story, don't you Fritz?' He was laughing now.

Fritz thought that Sapt had offended me, but I was not offended.

'So, the story of the scandal in my family is as famous here as it is in England!' I said with a smile.

'With that hair, I think everyone in Ruritania would know immediately that you're an Elphberg!' said Sapt.

---

1. **muttered:** 喃喃低語

I began to feel uncomfortable. If I I'd realised how similar I looked to the King's family, I wouldn't have travelled here. At this moment, a man's voice called from the forest. 'Fritz, Fritz, where are you man?'

Fritz von Tarlenheim looked worried, 'It's the King,' he said, but old Sapt laughed quietly to himself.

Then a young man jumped out from behind a tree, and when we saw each other we stared in total shock! Apart from a few unimportant details, the young man and I looked *exactly* the same. The new King of Ruritania could have been Rudolf Rassendyll, and I, Rudolf, could have been the King. For some time, we stood completely still looking at each other, then I remembered I was in front of the King. I took my hat off and bowed[1] to show my respect to him.

'Colonel – Fritz – who is this gentleman?' the King asked.

I was about to answer, when Colonel Sapt stepped between the King and me, and began to talk to His Majesty in a low growl[2]. The King kept looking at me, then he began to smile, his eyes lit up and he began to laugh so loudly the sound seemed to fill the entire forest. He came over to me. 'I'm happy to meet you, Cousin!' he said, putting his hand on my shoulder. 'What's your first name?'

'Rudolf,' I replied, 'the same as yours, Your Majesty[3]!'

The King put his arm through mine. 'Now, come and have dinner with us, I want to spend some time with you.'

1. **bowed:** 鞠躬
2. **growl:** 咆哮

3. **Your Majesty:** 國王或皇后陛下

Comprehension

1 **Now that you've read Chapter 1, answer the following questions.**

1 Who thinks Rudolf is wasting his life, and why?

_____

2 Who speaks fluent German, some French, Italian and Spanish?

_____

3 Who is going to become the next King of Ruritania, and when?

_____

4 Who does Rudolf first meet in Paris? What job does he do?

_____

5 Who travels on the same train to Dresden as Rudolf?

_____

6 Who is this person in love with? How is he related to the new King?

_____

2 **Rose won't be happy until Rudolf gets a job. In the space below, write a CV (Curriculum Vitae) for Rudolf, to help him. Remember to include information about what he can do, his previous experience and his character.**

Name	
Age	
Appearance	
Languages and other skills	
Hobbies	
Character	

Grammar

3 **There is a mistake in each of the following conditional sentences. Find the mistake, then correct the sentence.**

1 If I tell him I was going to Dresden, then my sister-in-law and brother would find out in less than a week!

_____

2 If the King had spent less time abroad, then more people recognise him!

_____

3 If the train leaves immediately, I wouldn't have gone to explore the forest.

_____

4 If I had realised how similar I looked to the King, I will not have come here.

_____

PRE-READING ACTIVITIES

Speaking

4 **Talk in pairs. What do you think has happened to the King, and what do you think will happen next? Use the words in the box to help you.**

> Black Michael • poisoned • Rudolf Rassendyll • wear the King's clothes • travel to Strelsau • coronation

The King was lying on the floor. His face was as red as his hair and he was breathing heavily. Sapt showed no respect towards the King, and kicked him hard, but he still did not move. His face and head were also wet with water.

Chapter Two

The King Keeps His Appointment

The King didn't stop talking while we walked. He wanted to hear about my family, and he laughed when I told him about the red-haired family portraits. He laughed even more loudly when I told him my journey to Ruritania was a secret from my family.

After half an hour, we reached a small hunting lodge[1] in the forest, where the King and his friends were staying. An old servant came out to us.

'Well, Josef,' said the King, 'is our dinner ready?'

Soon we had a simple but generous dinner. Sapt ate as though he hadn't eaten for weeks, Fritz ate delicately, and the King and I both ate a lot.

'Us Elphbergs have always liked our food,' he said, smiling at me.

'Remember tomorrow,' Fritz said, looking worried. It was getting late, and we were still talking and eating. Fritz tried to get us to go to bed, but after a while, he shrugged[2] and gave up, and joined in the conversation. The King talked about the future, old Sapt talked about the past, Fritz told us about a girl he was in love with, and I talked about the Elphbergs. We all talked at once until it was extremely late at night.

Then the King stopped talking and said, 'I believe I've eaten enough.'

At that moment, Josef brought out a wonderful cake. 'Your brother, the Duke of Strelsau, asked me to give you this cake,' he said. 'He sends it with his love.'

---

1. **hunting lodge:** 為狩獵者而設的小
旅館

2. **shrugged:** 聳肩

'Ah!' said the King, his eyes lighting up, 'Well done, Black Michael. Come on Josef, let me have that cake.' And he ate it without giving any of us a single piece!

❖ ❖ ❖

I didn't know whether I'd been asleep for a minute or a year. I woke up suddenly and felt very cold. My face, hair and clothes were covered in water. I opened my eyes and saw old Sapt opposite me. He had an unpleasant smile on his face and an empty bucket in his hand. Fritz von Tarlenheim sat at the table. He looked terribly pale and had black circles round his eyes.

I jumped to my feet angrily. 'What kind of a joke is this?'

'There's no time to argue,' Colonel Sapt replied, putting the bucket down, 'It was the only way we could wake you.'

'I don't see why you had to throw water over me.' I was very angry, and shivering with cold.

'Rassendyll,' Fritz interrupted me. 'Look here.'

The King was lying on the floor. His face was as red as his hair and he was breathing heavily. Sapt showed no respect towards the King, and kicked him hard, but the King still didn't move. His face and head were also wet with water.

'We've been trying to wake him for the last half hour,' said Fritz, shaking his head.

I went down on my knees and put my ear to the King's chest. His heart beat felt unnaturally slow and faint. We all looked at each other. 'Do you think that cake he ate, the one his brother sent, was poisoned?' I whispered.

'I don't know,' said Sapt.

'We must get a doctor for him!'

'There are none near here,' said Sapt.

'But the coronation!' I cried in horror.

Fritz shrugged his shoulders again, which I began to believe was a habit of his.

'Then we must tell everyone in Strelsau the King is ill,' I said.

'The problem is,' laughed Sapt, 'the people know all about his "illnesses", he's been "ill" before. If he doesn't go to his own coronation then people will start to think he doesn't want to be their King. Do we really think he was poisoned?' he asked.

Fritz and I both said yes.

'It was that evil man Black Michael,' said Fritz.

'I agree,' said Sapt, 'he wanted to stop Rudolf becoming King today. Rassendyll, you don't know Black Michael, but I do. He's simply waiting for the right time to take our King's place.'

Fritz put his head in his hands. The King breathed loudly, and Sapt kicked him again. We were all silent for a moment. Then Sapt looked at me for a long time. 'As a man grows old, he believes in Fate. Fate sent you here, and Fate sends you now to Strelsau,' he said thoughtfully. When I understood what he meant, I nearly fell over in shock. 'It's impossible,' I said, 'I'd be recognised in an instant!'

'It's a risk,' agreed Sapt, 'but you look so like him, I'm sure no one will suspect you're not the real King. Are you afraid?'

'What do you mean?'

'All our lives will be in danger if anyone recognises you, but if you don't go, then by tonight Black Michael will be the new King of Ruritania, and the real King will be in prison or dead.'

A minute went by in complete silence while I thought about the plan. Then I made my decision, but, before I could say

anything, Sapt took my hand and cried, 'Please tell me you'll go!'

I turned to look at the King lying on the floor, 'Yes I'll go,' I said.

Over the next hour we worked quickly. We picked up the King and carried him into a small room in the lodge. I got changed into the King's clothes, and Josef got the horses ready.

It was six o'clock in the morning when we left. The game had begun. How would it end? None of us could tell.

We arrived at the station and got onto the train. I looked at my watch – the King's watch – it was eight o'clock. The train left, and at around half-past nine, I saw the towers[1] and spires[2] of a great city.

'This is Strelsau, your capital city, Your Majesty,' said Sapt with a laugh. I felt nervous, but Sapt was more confident, 'You'll do,' he said. Then he said quietly, 'I pray to God that we're all still alive tonight.'

'So do I!' said Fritz.

The train stopped. Sapt and Fritz jumped out and held the door for me. I took a deep breath, and said a short prayer to God. Then I stepped onto the platform of the station at Strelsau.

A moment later, everyone started running around. Men ran up to greet me and ran off again; men took me to have breakfast; men rode off to tell everyone that I had arrived. Soon the church bells were ringing. I could hear military music, and men shouting their support for the King with cries of 'Long live the King!'

Old Sapt smiled. 'Long live both Kings!' he whispered to me.

Outside the station, Sapt introduced me to several important-looking people. There was the head of the army, Marshal Strakencz, and just behind him, the head politician, the Chancellor.

No one seemed to suspect that I wasn't the real King. This made me feel more confident. I began to feel much less nervous, and my heart stopped beating so hard.

---

1. **towers:** 高樓　　　　　　　　　　2. **spires:** 教堂尖頂

I got onto my horse, and we began our journey through Strelsau. At first, we passed through wide, modern streets, where the richer people lived. Then we reached the old heart of the city where the poor lived, and at last, we were at the cathedral. This was when the reality of the situation hit me. I couldn't believe what I was doing! I got off my horse and looked around, but my eyes saw nothing. I walked into the cathedral with everyone watching me, but I saw nothing of the crowd. The only two faces I saw inside the cathedral were a girl, pale and lovely, with that wonderful, red Elphberg hair, and a man whose red cheeks, black hair and dark eyes told me I was meeting my brother, Black Michael. He went pale. I think that until he actually saw me, he did not believe the King had really come to Strelsau at all!

Of what followed next I remember nothing. I think I knelt[1] at the front of the cathedral. The Cardinal, the head of the church, spoke, then I stood, and he put the crown of Ruritania on my head. Someone announced that I was King, and so I became King of Ruritania. Dear reader, I have a very lovely painting of the whole thing in my dining room at home. The portrait of the King is very good!

Then the lady with the pale face and wonderful hair stepped towards me.

'The Princess Flavia,' a man announced.

She took my hand and bent down to kiss it. I didn't know what to do, so I pulled her to me and kissed her on each cheek. She blushed[2] when I did that. Then came the Duke of Strelsau. He was trembling, and looked as though he wanted to run away. His hand was shaking so much it seemed to jump when he took my hand, and his lips felt dry when he kissed it.

I kissed him on the cheek. I think we were both glad when that was over! There was no doubt in his face, or in the face of the Princess, that I was the real King.

---

1. knelt: 跪下

2. blushed: 臉紅

Princess Flavia and I rode back on our horses through the crowds to the palace. I was in a difficult situation. I'd forgotten to ask Sapt what my relationship with my cousin was. She was so lovely, I could easily imagine that the King was in love with her, but I decided to say nothing. After a while, the Princess turned to me calmly.

'Do you know, Rudolf,' said she, 'you look somehow different today?'

I got rather worried when I heard that.

'You look calmer,' she continued, 'as though you are worried about something. Don't tell me becoming King has made you more serious at last?'

I wasn't sure what to say, so I answered. 'I try to do what makes you happy.' She blushed again, then I said. 'My dear cousin, this has been the most extraordinary day of my life.'

She smiled happily, then she looked more serious. 'Did you notice Michael?'

'Yes I did, he was *not* enjoying himself.'

'Do be careful of him!' she went on.

'Yes,' I said, 'He wants what I have, and,' I added, looking at her, 'he wants what I may have one day.'

She understood that I was talking about her, but she said nothing.

When we arrived at the palace, we heard loud guns and more military music. Servants stood on either side of the wide stairs as we went up. Then, as King, I went into the royal palace. I sat at my great table, with the Cardinal on my left, my cousin on my right and, on her other side, Black Michael. Sapt stood behind my chair, and I saw Fritz von Tarlenheim looking nervous. I wondered what the real King of Ruritania was doing.

At the end of the day, Fritz, Sapt and I went to the King's rooms in the palace. We were exhausted.

'Are you ready to leave?' asked Sapt.

'Yes,' I said, with a sigh. 'Soon, I'll be Rudolf Rassendyll again.'

'You'll be lucky if you are even that,' Sapt said. 'Every minute we stay in Strelsau, the more likely we are to lose our heads.'

The plan was for me and Sapt to leave the palace by a secret door, and go back to the King at Zenda. Then I would ride through the night to the Ruritanian border and escape.

We rode quickly and were nearly at Zenda, when we heard two men behind us. We got off our horses and hid in the forest near the road. It was night now, but the moon shone so brightly that the road looked white. As the horses got nearer, I saw who it was.

'It's the Duke!' I said.

It was Black Michael and one of his servants. They rode past us towards the Castle of Zenda.

When we arrived back at the hunting lodge that we had left only that morning, it was dark and no one came out to us. We went inside, and stopped in front of the room where we had left the King. Sapt gave a shout and pointed at the ground. Blood was spreading under the door.

I found a candle and lit it, then I opened the door and went in. I followed the blood, holding the candle high above my head. In a corner, I saw the body of a man lying on his back, with a deep red cut across his throat. It was the old servant, Josef.

I felt a hand on my shoulders. It was Sapt, and he was looking terrified.

'The King? My God! The King?' he whispered.

I threw the light around the room.

'The King,' I said, 'is not here.'

Reading Comprehension

1 Choose the correct answer.

1 The King cannot go to the coronation because...

A ☐ he's too tired.

B ☐ he's been killed.

C ☐ he's been poisoned.

2 When Rudolf Rassendyll wakes up, he feels...

A ☐ tired and unhappy.

B ☐ cold and angry.

C ☐ alone and frightened.

3 When Rudolf arrives in Strelsau...

A ☐ everyone can see he's not the real King.

B ☐ everyone seems afraid of him.

C ☐ everyone treats him as if he were the real King.

4 When Rudolf gets to the cathedral, he...

A ☐ can't believe what's happening to him.

B ☐ feels confident and relaxed.

C ☐ recognises lots of people in the crowd.

5 When 'King' Rudolf kisses Princess Flavia, she...

A ☐ goes down on her knees and kisses his feet.

B ☐ announces that he's the King.

C ☐ is embarrassed, and goes red.

6 When Michael comes to greet the new King, he...

A ☐ is trembling with excitement.

B ☐ is shaking and unhappy.

C ☐ kisses his dear brother with affection.

2 Put the events in Chapter 2 in the correct order. The first two have been done to help you.

- [ ] Rudolf kisses Princess Flavia and his brother Michael.
- [2] The King is poisoned.
- [ ] Rudolf, Sapt and Fritz travel to Strelsau.
- [ ] Rudolf and Flavia travel by horse to the royal palace.
- [ ] Rudolf is crowned King of Ruritania.
- [ ] Rudolf Rassendyll puts the King's clothes on.
- [7] The King eats a cake sent by Black Michael.
- [ ] Rudolf rides to the cathedral.

Vocabulary

3 Choose the correct adverb from the box to complete the sentences below.

excitedly • loudly • nervously • suspiciously • unpleasantly

1 The King laughed _____ , when I told him my journey was a secret.

2 When I woke, Sapt was smiling at me _____ .

3 Everyone will recognise me, I thought _____ .

4 No one looked at me _____ .

5 The people of Ruritania greeted their new King _____ .

PRE-READING ACTIVITIES

Speaking

4 Talk in pairs. What do you think will happen next, answer T or F. Then read the next chapter. Were you right? Did anything surprise you?

	T	F
1 The King has been killed.	[ ]	[ ]
2 Black Michael's men will capture Rudolf.	[ ]	[ ]
3 Sapt and Rudolf will kill Michael.	[ ]	[ ]
4 Rudolf will fall in love with Flavia.	[ ]	[ ]
5 Antoinette de Mauban will betray Rudolf.	[ ]	[ ]
6 Rudolf will be attacked by some of Michael's men.	[ ]	[ ]

Chapter Three

A New Use for a Tea Table

I put my arm round Sapt and helped him out of the room. For ten minutes or more we sat silent in the dining room. Then Sapt dried the tears from his eyes, breathed deeply, and was himself again. It was one o'clock in the morning.

'They've got the King!' he said, stamping[1] his foot on the floor.

'Yes,' I said, 'and we must get back to Strelsau immediately. We must tell the army to come and rescue the King.'

Sapt said nothing.

'The King may be murdered while we sit here!' I continued. I couldn't understand why Sapt wasn't doing anything. Then a large smile appeared on his face. 'Don't worry,' he said, 'the King will be in his capital again tomorrow.'

'The King?' I asked.

'The King who was crowned yesterday!'

I began to understand his plan. He put his hand on my shoulder. 'Young man, if you can be the King for a little longer, I think you might be able to save the real King's life!'

'But Black Michael knows I'm not the real King,' I said. 'All the men who have taken the King know I'm not the real King…'

'Yes, but they can't say "This is not the King, because we kidnapped

1. **stamping:** 頓腳

the King and murdered his servant." Can they say that? No, because then everyone would know what they've done.'

I saw what he meant. Black Michael couldn't say who I really was without showing everyone the real King.

'What if they've already killed him?' I asked.

'Well, then you'll have to be the King of Ruritania forever! But I don't believe they'll kill him.'

I was young then, and loved adventure. I was being offered a chance that perhaps no one else has ever had. 'Sapt,' I cried...

'Excellent! Now let's go,' he said before I could finish.

We were about to leave the house, when Sapt pulled me back from the door. Coming along the road were seven or eight men.

'I think they've come to bury Josef,' said Sapt.

I thought about poor Josef, who had given his life to save his King.

'Colonel Sapt, shall we punish them for killing Josef?' I asked.

Sapt thought for a moment. 'It's dangerous, but, why not?'

We went to the back of the house and got new horses. Sapt took his gun out, and I got my sword. We waited a moment, then Sapt cried, 'Now!' and we rode round the house. Sapt shot one of them and I killed another. They started shooting back at us, but we laughed and rode quickly away. As we got closer to Strelsau, though, the excitement of the fight disappeared, and we rode in silence.

Back at the palace, we went through the secret door to Fritz. When he saw us, he cried. 'Where's the King? *Where's* the King?'

'Be quiet, you idiot,' whispered Sapt, 'Not so loud! This *is* the King!'

Fritz whispered, 'Is the King dead?'

'No, I don't think he is!' I replied, 'but Black Michael has got him!'

The next day, for three hours, Sapt told me about my duties as King. After that, I had a quick breakfast, spent another three hours with the Chancellor, then the French Ambassador was introduced. Over the next few days, I met all the important people who had come to meet the new King! Then, at last, we were left alone.

Fritz was becoming impatient. 'Are we going to do nothing? We should be helping the King,' he said.

'We're going to do nothing *stupid*,' growled Sapt, annoyed with Fritz.

I tried to explain. 'I cannot tell people what Michael has done without everyone finding out who I really am. And Michael cannot tell everyone who I am, because everyone will know what he's done!'

Fritz nodded, then he asked Sapt. 'Did you know that half of the Six are in Strelsau?'

Sapt looked suddenly excited. 'Only half of them? Are you sure?'

Fritz nodded again.

'Then we can be sure that the King is still alive. If three of the Six are here, then the other three are guarding him!'

'Yes, – I believe you're right,' said Fritz, and he began to smile.

'Gentlemen, gentlemen!' I said, 'Who are "the Six"?'

'They are six men who work for Black Michael. There are three Ruritanians; then there's a Frenchman, a Belgian, and one of your countrymen,' explained Sapt. 'I'm sure you will meet them soon!'

❖ ❖ ❖

Fritz and I decided I should visit the Princess. We had to make sure that she loved the King enough to marry him one day. But I, Rudolf Rassendyll, couldn't fall in love with her. This was the most difficult part, because I think she was the most beautiful woman I've ever seen!

When we arrived, I was shown into the Princess's private room, while Fritz waited outside.

'You're like the prince in Shakespeare,' she said, when she saw me, 'who's made better by becoming a king! I'm proud of you Rudolf, yes, even your face seems different.'

I thanked her, but quickly changed the subject.

'I hear that my brother Michael is in Strelsau,' I said.

'Yes, he is here,' she said, frowning[1] a little.

At that moment, we heard shouts from the street. The Princess ran to the window. 'It's him!' she cried. 'The Duke's coming here!'

When Michael arrived, he was frowning and seemed angry.

'Brother,' I said, kissing him, 'I'm pleased to see you.'

He thanked me coldly. He couldn't hide his feelings – anyone could have seen how much he hated me, and hated me even more because I was with Princess Flavia! We talked for a while in the Princess's room, until Michael suddenly stood up and said, 'There are three friends of mine who'd like to meet you, Your Majesty.'

I put my arm in his and we went out of the room together. The look on his face was honey to me!

'These gentlemen,' said Michael, 'are your most loyal servants, and my very good friends.'

The first was the Frenchman, De Gautet, next came the Belgian, Bersonin, and last, the Englishman, Detchard. They greeted me politely, and when they left, I went back to my cousin. She was standing by the door. I took her hand and said goodbye.

'Rudolf,' she said, very low, 'be careful, won't you?'

When I saw her beautiful face so full of concern for me, I couldn't speak. I kissed her hand, and left to find Fritz.

A day later, Sapt arrived, carrying a letter. 'It looks like a woman's writing,' he said, 'But first I have news for you. The King's at the Castle of Zenda.'

1. frowning: 皺眉

'How do you know?'

'Because the other half of Michael's Six are there – Lauengram, Krafstein and the worst of the lot, Rupert Hentzau. Now, read the letter,' he said. I opened it.

> At the end of New Street is a garden with a wall round it. At twelve o'clock tonight, the King must go through the gate in the wall, and come to a summerhouse[1] with six steps. There he will discover something important.

I did not trust the letter, but then I saw something written on the back.

> If you do not believe me, the writer continued, ask Colonel Sapt which woman wants to stop the Duke marrying Princess Flavia. And ask if her name begins with A–.

I jumped to my feet.

'Good God! It's Antoinette de Mauban,' I cried, and I told Sapt about the lady I had seen with George Featherly at the station in Paris.

❖ ❖ ❖

It was half-past eleven when Sapt and I got to the gate in the wall. Sapt waited there, while I went through and found the summerhouse. I went up the six steps, and pushed open the old door. A woman rushed over and took my hand. 'Shut the door,' she whispered.

There was a candle burning in the summerhouse, and I saw she was wearing a beautiful evening dress. Next to her, were a couple of chairs and a small metal table.

'Don't talk,' she said, 'we don't have time. I know you, Mr

---

1. summerhouse: 花園涼亭

Rassendyll. The Duke told me to write that letter. In twenty minutes, three men will be here to kill you. They'll leave your body in a dark street. Black Michael will take your friends, Colonel Sapt and Fritz von Tarlenheim, and the real King will be killed. Then he'll announce he's the new King, or the Princess will become Queen, then he'll marry her and become King anyway.'

'Madame, thank you. Where in the castle is the King?'

'Across the drawbridge you come to a heavy door, behind that is… Listen, What's that?'

There were steps outside.

'They're coming! They're too soon!' and she turned as pale as death.

'I think they've arrived at exactly the right time!' I said. I blew out the candle, and looked through a small hole in the door. On the lowest step I saw three men. I pulled out my gun and told Antoinette to move away from the door.

'Mr Rassendyll, we have an offer for you,' said a voice in perfect English. 'Will you promise not to shoot until we've finished talking?' It was Detchard, one of Black Michael's Six. The three men came up two more steps. All three had their guns pointing at the door.

'Will you let us in?' Detchard continued.

'We can speak through the door,' I said.

'Will you promise not to shoot while we talk?'

'I promise not to shoot before you do,' I said. 'But I won't let you in. Stand outside.'

The three walked up the last step and stood by the door.

'Well, gentlemen, what's your offer?' I asked.

'We'll take you to the border, and give you fifty thousand English pounds.'

Antoinette shook her head. 'You *cannot* trust them.'

I picked up the little metal table and held it front of me to protect me from their guns. In this way, I had my head and chest completely covered by the table. When I was ready, I said. 'Gentlemen, I accept your offer,' and pretended to open the door. 'I can't open it!' I cried, 'It's stuck!'

'Let me do it,' said Detchard, impatiently.

The door was pulled open. At that moment, I gave a loud yell, and rushed at them like a wild animal. Three shots hit the table, but I didn't stop. I ran straight into them and caught them all fully in the chest. They fell down shouting and waving their arms about. I and the table carried on running down the steps. Antoinette de Mauban shrieked[1], but I rose to my feet[2], laughing. De Gautet and Bersonin lay on the ground. Detchard stood up and took another shot at me, which missed, and I shot him back. Then I ran as fast as I could. Hearing steps behind me I turned and fired again. The steps stopped. I ran back to Sapt who had gone mad with worry. I put my hand on his shoulder and said, 'Come home, old friend, I have the best story to tell you about four men round a tea table!'

I hope that you noticed, dear reader, I kept my promise? I didn't fire my gun until they'd fired at me!

---

1. shrieked: 尖叫   2. rose to my feet: 站起來

Characters

1 **Who am I? Describe the following characters. Use what you have learnt in the story so far. The first one has been done as an example.**

   1 Antoinette de Mauban *beautiful lady from Paris, in love with Duke Michael, helps Rudolf because she doesn't want Michael to marry Flavia*

   2 Black Michael _____

   3 Colonel Sapt _____

   4 Princess Flavia _____

   5 Rudolf Rassendyll _____

   6 The Six _____

2 **Where am I in Chapter 3? Match the person or people to the places in the list below. (Some of the characters may be in more than one place!)**

> Antoinette de Mauban • Bersonin • Black Michael
> • Colonel Sapt •Detchard • De Gautet • Josef • The King •
> Princess Flavia • Rudolf Rassendyll

   1 At the little house in the forest of Zenda

   _____ _____ _____

   2 At the castle in Zenda _____

   3 In Flavia's private room

   _____ _____ _____

   4 Waiting outside the gate at the house in New Street _____

   5 Inside the summerhouse

   _____ _____

   6 Outside the door of the summerhouse _____

   _____ _____

   7 Hiding behind a metal table _____

Grammar for First

3 **Fill in the gaps with the word you think fits best. Only one word is needed for each gap. The first has been done as an example.**

The door was pulled (**1**) ____*open*____. At that moment, I gave a loud yell, and rushed (**2**) _____ them (**3**) _____ a wild animal. Three shots hit (**4**) _____ table, but I didn't stop. I ran straight (**5**) _____ them and caught (**6**) _____ all fully in the chest. They fell (**7**) _____ shouting and waving their arms (**8**) _____. I and the table carried (**9**) _____ running (**10**) _____ the steps. Antoinette de Mauban shrieked, (**11**) _____ I stood (**12**) _____ laughing.

Speaking

4 **What do you think of Rudolf Rassendyll? How would you describe his character after the events in Chapter 3? If you met him, do you think you'd like him?**

PRE-READING ACTIVITIES

Listening

5 **Look at the following verb phrases. Use a dictionary to help you with any words that you do not know. Then listen to the extract from Chapter 4, and tick the phrases as you hear them.**

- ☐ was playing cards with
- ☐ Sapt came in with the police report
- ☐ the people are disappointed that
- ☐ haven't got engaged to
- ☐ that's the first I've heard of it!
- ☐ you must make her believe you're in love with her

Chapter Four

An Impossible Choice

3 On the evening after my adventure at the summerhouse, I was playing cards with Fritz von Tarlenheim, when Sapt came in with the police report as he did every day.

'This report is particularly interesting,' he said, sitting down. 'The Duke of Strelsau has left the city with De Gautet, Bersonin and Detchard. Madame de Mauban also left the city by train.

'The last thing is this – the people are disappointed that you haven't got engaged to the Princess yet. They're saying she might marry Michael. So, you're giving a party tonight, in honour of the Princess.'

'Well, that's the first I've heard of it,' I said, and Fritz laughed.

'Fritz has arranged everything. But tonight you must make her believe you're in love with her,' said Sapt.

'Do you really think it would be so difficult for me to fall in love with her?'

Fritz shook his head. 'No, I think it would be very easy,' he said. 'I also believe that the Princess has become very fond of the King since the coronation, and is upset that you haven't been to see her.'

'I think you must ask her to marry you tonight,' said Sapt.

This was terrible. I would be asking her to marry me, when she didn't know who who I really was. The other problem was that I, Rudolf Rassendyll, could never hope to marry her.

THE PRISONER OF ZENDA

'I won't do anything to hurt the Princess,' I said, angrily.

'All right,' said Sapt, with his clever smile, 'just do what you can.'

Sapt must have known how unhappy all this would make the Princess, but that didn't seem important to him. I think he wanted me to be King of Ruritania forever if we lost the real King!

The party was unforgettable. The Princess and I started the dancing, and everyone was looking at us and talking about us. After the dancing, we went in to supper. I was finding things difficult by then. I had looked into her eyes, and seen that she truly loved me. She was nervous, and I could hardly speak.

After the meal, she took my arm and we walked down to a little room, where coffee was served to us. At last we were alone.

The room had large windows that were open onto the garden. Flavia sat down and I stood opposite her. She looked at me, full of love, then she blushed. Ah, if you had seen her! At that moment, I forgot the King in Zenda, I forgot the King in Strelsau. She was a Princess and I was an ordinary man, but do you think I remembered that? I knelt in front of her, took her hand, and kissed it.

She pushed me away. 'Do you really love me, or are you only doing this because you have to?'

'It's true!' I said, 'True that I love you more than life!'

'Oh, if you were not the King, then I could show you how I love you. How is it that I love you now, Rudolf, when I didn't before you became King?' When Flavia said this, I knew it was me, Rudolf Rassendyll, that she loved.

'So you didn't love me before the coronation?' I asked.

She laughed, 'You speak as if you'd be pleased to hear me say "Yes" to that. But yes, it's true, I didn't love you before.'

Here was my chance to tell her the truth. 'If I weren't the King, but an ordinary man…' Before I could finish, she put her hand in mine.

'If you were a convict[1] in the prison of Strelsau, you would be *my* king,' she said.

At that moment, there was a sound in the garden and Sapt appeared at the window. I couldn't finish what I'd been going to say! I don't know how long he'd been listening, but he'd come in at exactly the right moment to stop me telling Flavia the truth.

'A thousand apologies,' he said, 'but the Cardinal is waiting to say goodbye to you, Your Majesty.'

We went back to the party – everyone was looking at me, smiling and whispering. I knew Sapt had been spreading the news that, one day soon, Princess Flavia and I would be married.

It was three in the morning when I got back to my room. Sapt sat with me and I stared at the fire. On the table was a rose that Flavia had given me. Sapt was looking at it, as if he was about to pick it up.

'That's mine,' I said, putting my hand on it, 'not yours, or the King's.'

'I think we did some good work for the King tonight,' he said.

I looked at him angrily. 'What's to stop me doing some good work for myself?' I said. 'I won't treat Flavia like this. If we wait any longer to save the King, then we *will* have a problem. I could send both Michael and his brother to their deaths, then I could marry the Princess and remain King of Ruritania.'

'I am sure you're right,' said Sapt, smiling calmly at me.

'Let's go to Zenda,' I cried, 'and get the real King back as quickly as possible, before it's too late.'

He put his hand on my shoulder and said, 'Before God, you're the best Elphberg I have ever known!'

It was the most difficult decision of my life. I loved Flavia, but I

---

1. convict: 囚犯

had to save the King and I had to make sure that Michael didn't kill him before I could rescue him.

It was a fine, bright morning when I walked to the Princess's palace, alone. I was carrying a bunch of pretty flowers in my hand. The more I loved her, the more I suffered, but I knew what I was doing would help the King. You see, the Princess was very popular with the people, and they wanted her to marry the King, but, above all, I *had* to stop Michael from marrying her.

When I arrived I found Helga, one of the Princess's friends, in the garden. There was a window open above our heads.

'Madame, you have a visitor,' Helga called up, happily.

Flavia looked out of the window, and blew me a kiss. 'Bring the King up, Helga; I'll give him some coffee,' she called out.

Helga took me to Flavia's room, and when we were alone we greeted each other as lovers do. Then she gave me two letters to read. One was from Black Michael. It was an invitation for her to spend the day with him, as she did every year, at the Castle of Zenda. I threw the letter down in disgust. Flavia laughed at me, and then looking more serious, pointed at the next letter. 'I don't know who that comes from,' she said. I recognised the writing immediately. It was from Antoinette de Mauban.

Princess Flavia, I have no reason to help you, the letter read, *but I would do anything to stop you falling into the power of the Duke. Accept no invitations from him, and do not go anywhere without a large guard.*

Flavia asked. 'Do you think it's a joke?'

'No, I don't,' I answered. 'The letter is from a good friend, an unhappy woman who I know. Please don't go to Zenda, Flavia, tell the Duke that you're ill.'

With that, I left her and went to see Marshal Strakencz, the head of the army in Strelsau. I liked him and, most importantly, I trusted him. I needed someone to defend the city and the woman I loved more than anyone in the world. I told the Marshal to let no one from the Duke come near the Princess.

'I think you might be right to be suspicious, Your Majesty,' he said, and shook his head with a sigh.

'Marshal, I'm leaving Strelsau for a few days. Every evening, I'll send a message to you. If my messenger[1] doesn't come for three days, you must tell Michael you want to speak to the King. If he doesn't bring you the King in twenty-four hours, then you'll know that the King is dead. You know who must become queen if the King is dead?'

The Marshal nodded. Princess Flavia,' he said.

'Then promise me that you will protect Flavia to the death, kill Michael, and make her queen after me.'

'I promise on my life!'

I held my hand out to him. 'Marshal, in the next few days you may hear strange things about the man who stands in front of you. Do you think he has been a good king?'

'I think you have been a wise king,' the old man said, and a brave man. You have been a true gentleman to your people, and to the Princess Flavia.'

I was very touched by his words.

When I got back, Fritz and Sapt told everyone we were going hunting in Zenda the next morning. Soon, everything was ready, and there was only one thing left to do – I had to go and see Flavia one last time.

The people called out to me happily as I rode through the streets,

---

1. **messenger:** 信差

but my heart was breaking. No one knew how I suffered! They hadn't looked into Flavia's eyes and seen what I'd seen, but, although I felt depressed, I made an effort to smile and wave. When I arrived, though, Flavia was distant and cold. 'I'm sorry there's nothing to interest you in Strelsau,' she said, tapping[1] her foot on the floor. 'Stupidly, I thought you wanted to spend time with me, but I see that hunting is more important to you.'

'Yes, there are a lot of wild animals at Zenda!' I said. I began to play with her hair, but she pushed me away.

'Are you really angry with me?' I asked.

'You told me last night that every hour away from me was wasted. But of course, that isn't important compared to hunting!' There were tears in her eyes.

'Why are you crying?' I asked.

'Because this is what you used to be like,' she said, 'before the Coronation,' she said, 'This is not like the King I have come to love!'

With a loud sigh, I pulled her to me, and told her the real reason I was leaving. 'My love! Did you honestly believe that I was going hunting in the forest? No, I'm going to hunt Michael in his castle at Zenda.' She went very pale when she heard this.

'I promise to come back soon, and I'll send you all my heart every day,' I told her.

'You'll not be in any danger, Rudolf, will you?'

'I'll try not to be,' I promised.

'Oh, please don't stay away long! I won't be able to sleep until you're back.'

'I don't know when I'll be back,' I answered, 'but if I don't come back, then you must take my place, you must become queen. You're the last of the real Elphbergs.'

1. tapping: 輕敲

'I will! I'll do that, although my life will be empty and my heart will be dead,' she said, holding onto me.

'Oh, you'll see me once more before I die!' I said, without thinking.

'What do you mean?' she asked. She was starting to cry, but I couldn't tell her what I meant, I couldn't tell her who I really was.

'How could I not return to the loveliest lady in the world?' I said, drying her tears. 'A thousand Michaels couldn't stop me from coming back to you.'

When she heard that, she seemed a little happier. 'You won't let Michael hurt you?'

'No, my love, I won't,' I answered.

'You won't let anyone take you away from me?'

Again I answered, 'No, my love.'

But it wasn't true. There was one person who would keep me from her, and I didn't mean Michael. The person who would keep me from her was the person I was risking my life for – the King. If he lived, then he would be with her and I would not.

As I kissed her, I saw again the young man I had met in the forest of Zenda. I remembered him lying on the floor, after he'd been poisoned with the cake Michael had sent. I almost imagined him standing between me and the woman I held in my arms, the woman who looked at me with such love. Reader, her beautiful eyes haunt me even now, and will until the day I die.

Reading Comprehension

1a **Answer the following questions.**

1 Why have Sapt and Fritz organised a party in honour of the Princess? _____

2 What does Sapt want Rudolf to do at the party? _____
_____

3 What does Rudolf discover about Flavia during the party?
_____

4 How does Rudolf know that the Princess is in love with him and not the King? _____
_____

5 What happens just as Rudolf is about to tell Flavia the truth?
_____

6 Why does Rudolf say they cannot wait any longer to save the King? _____
_____

7 Why is Flavia upset that Rudolf is going hunting?_____
_____

8 What three things does Rudolf ask Marshal Strakencz to do?
_____

1b **In this chapter, Rudolf is tempted to marry Flavia and forget about the King at Zenda. Do you think he was right to make the decision he did? What would you have done in his place?**

Summary Writing

2 **Write a short summary of what happens at the party. Remember to include details about Rudolf and Flavia, but also about Sapt and the other guests.**

_____
_____

Word Formation for First

3 **Read the following text. Use the correct form of the word in brackets to complete the gaps. The first one has been done as an example.**

I was in an (**1**) ___*impossible*___ (possible) situation. The Princess was the (**2**) _____ (lovely) woman I had ever met, and, because I am a gentleman, I hate being (**3**) _____ (honest), but telling her the (**4**) _____ (true) would have been too (**5**) _____ (danger). In fact, the situation turned me into a complete (**6**) _____ (lie)! We were (**7**) _____ (love), but we could never be together! And the (**8**) _____ (bad) part of it was, that I had promised to save the man who would take her from me forever!

PRE-READING ACTIVITIES

Listening

▶ 4   **4** **In Chapter 5 we meet a new character – Rupert Hentzau. Listen to the extract and underline the word or phrase below that best describes Rupert. What impression do you get of Rupert?**

1 rides a powerful horse/arrives on foot
2 wears fine clothes/wears old clothes
3 likeable/arrogant
4 handsome/ugly
5 young/middle aged
6 always looks angry/smiles a lot
7 charming/rude
8 a good person/a bad person

Chapter Five

An Evil Plan

About five kilometres from Zenda, on the opposite side of the valley from the Duke's castle, stands a modern chateau. It belongs to a cousin of Fritz von Tarlenheim, who was happy for us to stay there.

Our servants and bags left Strelsau early in the morning. At midday, we took the train for thirty kilometres, then rode the rest of the way. With me were Sapt and Fritz, and ten other gentlemen who were loyal to the King. Sapt and Fritz told them about the attack on me at the summerhouse. They also told them that a friend of the King's was being held prisoner at the Castle of Zenda, and that rescuing him was the reason we'd come to stay nearby. We could not tell them everything, but they trusted us. They were brave and young, and ready to defend the King.

Now that we'd left Strelsau, I had to forget about the Princess. I could only think about getting the King out of the castle alive. I had to admit the situation looked impossible. We couldn't simply attack the castle, we had to find a cleverer way of rescuing the King. Michael would know that we hadn't really come here to hunt, but I thought I might have one advantage. Because Michael was so dishonest himself, he would never believe I would give up the crown *and* the Princess to help the King. I think he really was in love with Flavia, and I almost felt sorry for him. I knew he wouldn't think twice before killing his brother, but I didn't think he would do it yet. If his brother was dead, then I would become King of Ruritania forever, and he would lose everything. No, he'd try to kill Rudolf Rassendyll first, and only then kill the King.

▶ 4   I hadn't been at the chateau for more than an hour, when Michael sent us some unwelcome visitors. The other three of his famous Six arrived on powerful horses and wearing fine clothes. It was the three Ruritanian gentlemen – Lauengram, Krafstein and Rupert Hentzau. Rupert Hentzau, who looked around twenty-three or twenty-four years old, came forward. He told me that my *loving* brother was sorry not to come and see me himself, but he and a number of his servants had a serious illness. Rupert gave me an arrogant[1] smile. He was a handsome devil!

'I hope he's not too ill?' I said, 'And what about my good friends De Gautet, Bersonin and Detchard? I hope they're well.'

Lauengram and Krafstein looked uncomfortable, but Rupert smiled even more. 'Detchard has recently been injured, Your Majesty. Someone shot him at a summerhouse, but he hopes to find whoever did it and kill him,' he answered.

I burst out laughing. I knew the name of that man! 'Well,' I said. 'I hope we meet again soon.'

Rupert and the other two left. If you have to have an enemy, I thought, then Rupert was a very charming one to have!

❖ ❖ ❖

That evening, Fritz and I rode to the small hotel that I'd visited on my first night in Ruritania.

'Fritz,' I said, 'there's a young girl at this little hotel. When we get there, I want you to go in and tell her we're two servants of the King.

1. arrogant: 高傲

Then I want you to order a private room and dinner for us both.'

When we arrived at the hotel, I pretended to be ill, and covered my face with a scarf. Fritz ordered dinner, and we went into the private dining room.

The girl arrived with the wine, then I took off my scarf. She looked at me and gave a shriek. 'Oh, I knew it was the King who'd been here the day before the coronation,' she said, excitedly. 'I'm sorry we didn't recognise you that day. I must go and tell Mother.'

'Please bring our dinner to us,' I said, 'but don't tell anyone that the King is here.'

She nodded, and was soon back with our dinner.

'How's Johann?' I asked her about the young man I'd met at the hotel that first night.

'Oh, we don't see him much, Your Majesty. He's busy at the castle now. There are no women up there, except one lady, so Johann has to look after them all.'

'Do you wish to serve the King?' I asked, and she nodded. Then tell Johann to meet you two miles out of Zenda tomorrow evening at ten o'clock. Say you'll be there and will walk home with him. Now, leave us,' I said, giving her a large amount of money as a thank you, 'and remember, don't tell anyone that the King has been here tonight.'

We ate, then I hid behind my scarf again and we went out to our horses. It was only half past eight, and the streets of Zenda were full of people gossiping about the King staying on one side of the town, and the Duke on the other!

When we got back to the chateau, Sapt ran out to us. 'Thank God you're safe,' he cried. 'Did you see them?'

'Who?' we asked.

'You mustn't ride around here without taking at least six men with you. One of your men has been shot through the arm, but I think it was really you they wanted to kill!'

'I'm sure you're right, Sapt,' I said. 'First points go to brother Michael!'

❖ ❖ ❖

The next morning, I was sitting quite happily in the sunshine in the garden, while one of my friends sang love songs. At that moment, young Rupert Hentzau came riding up to the chateau as if it belonged to him. He didn't seem at all worried about his own safety! He told me he had a private message for me from the Duke. I made everyone leave, and then he sat down beside me.

'The King is in love, it seems?' he said. I didn't reply. 'Come, Rassendyll, we're alone now. You don't need to pretend to be the King with me.'

'I do,' I answered, beginning to feel angry, 'because for the moment I *am* the King, and you'll speak to me as if I were the King.' He really was the most arrogant young man!

'If you say so. I was only being friendly, because I like you,' he said with a smile.

'What's the message from the Duke?' I asked, impatiently.

'The Duke offers you more than I would,' he growled. 'He'll give you as much money as you can carry, and will see you safely to the border.'

One look at my face told him my answer.

'So you refuse? I told Michael you wouldn't accept his offer,' and he gave me his most charming smile. 'Michael doesn't understand you as well as I do.'

I laughed then, but asked more seriously, 'So, how is your prisoner?'

'Well, he's alive,' and he shrugged.

We both stood up. Then, he said, 'And the pretty Princess? What a shame you will never marry her. In any case, I am sure she will be much happier married to Michael.'

'Go now,' I said, furiously, 'before I kill you.'

Then came the most audacious[1] thing I have known in my life. Rupert called for his horse. I stood in front of him, not suspecting anything, but in that instant I saw him pull out his sword to attack me. I moved out of the way as quickly as I could, but the sword caught my shoulder. If I hadn't moved, the sword would have hit my heart! I cried out and fell backwards onto the ground. Rupert pulled himself up onto his horse and galloped[2] away, with my friends shooting and shouting at him, but he was too fast for them. Then I fainted.

❖ ❖ ❖

I was put to bed, and lay there semi-conscious for many hours. It was night time before I had recovered enough to know where I was, though I was still weak and very tired, but Fritz was sitting next to my bed. He told me not to worry, the injury was not so bad, and he thought I would recover soon. He gave me another piece of good news. Johann had gone to meet the girl from the hotel and had been captured.

'I think he was almost glad that we'd taken him,' said Fritz, 'He thinks that when this is all over, Michael will kill everyone who knows the truth about what happened to the King, except for the Six of course.'

I ordered Johann to be brought to me at once. He came in with Sapt, looking angry and afraid. I ordered his hands to be untied, and told him to come and sit in a chair by my bed. I promised him whatever

1. **audacious:** 令人驚訝的　　　　　　2. **galloped:** 疾馳

he wanted if he would help us. I can tell you, dear reader, that he now lives as a wealthy man, but I am not allowed to tell you where!

We soon found out that Johann didn't agree with what the Duke was doing to the King. He'd been careful, though, to make sure the Duke trusted him enough to let him know his plans. This is what he told us.

'At the end of the drawbridge in the old part of the castle,' Johann said, 'there are some stone steps. At the bottom of these are two small rooms. The first is where the Six stay – three during the day, the other three at night. The King is being held in the second room. This has a small window overlooking the moat, but it has been covered up by a large pipe. If there is an attack on the first room, then one of the three will go immediately into the second room and kill the King.'

'What about the King's body?' I asked.

'Duke Michael has thought of that,' said Johann. 'While two of the Six defend the first room, the one who has killed the King opens the window and drops his body down the pipe. It will fall straight into the moat without being seen by anyone. But all this will only happen if everything else fails. He wants to kill you first, and then kill the King.'

Then came the cleverest part of the plan. Once the King had been killed and his body thrown into the moat, one of the Six would be tied up in the second room. If anyone came in demanding to know who was being held prisoner in the Castle of Zenda, Michael had invented a story. This false prisoner was a friend of his who had made him angry. He would publicly forgive the man, then let him go and tell everyone this was what had started the rumours about a Prisoner of Zenda. The visitors would leave and Michael would remove the King's body from the moat.

'Michael would kill me,' said Johann, desperately, 'if he knew what I'd told you. Please, please protect me!'

When he'd finished, Sapt, Fritz and I looked at each other in horror. Whatever we did, whether we attacked in secret, or with a large army, the result would always be the same – the King would be dead before we could get near him. If Michael beat us, then that was the end of me, but if I beat Michael, then I would still be King of Ruritania. (Of course, I would be able to marry Flavia then, and I rather liked that idea!) But, at some time in the future, Michael would try again to remove me.

'Does the King know all this?' I asked Johann.

'Yes, he does,' replied Johann, 'I was giving the King his dinner one day, when he asked Rupert Hentzau about the pipe. Rupert laughed, and said, "It's like Jacob's Ladder[1], only better, because the pipe will be more private than Jacob's Ladder – no one will be able to stare at you on your way to heaven!" When he heard what the pipe was for, the King went pale.' Johann shook his head. 'It's not easy to sleep in the Castle of Zenda, because they wouldn't think twice about cutting a man's throat. Rupert Hentzau is the worst; for him, killing people is a hobby.'

I told Fritz to take Johann away, then I looked at Sapt. 'This is impossibly difficult,' I said.

'It is,' he agreed, 'So difficult that I think you'll be King of Ruritania for another year!'

I lay back on my bed. 'I can see only two ways for the King to come out of Zenda alive. The first is by persuading one of the Duke's people to betray[2] him.'

'Well, that'll never happen!' Sapt interrupted.

'I hope you're wrong,' I said, 'because the second way I was going to say, is by a miracle from heaven!'

---

1. Jacob's Ladder: 來自聖經，雅各夢到人死後可
通往上帝的天梯

2. betray: 出賣

Reading Comprehension

1 Choose the correct answer.

1 Rudolf thinks that Michael won't kill the King yet. Why?

A ☐ Michael is too scared to kill his own brother.

B ☐ Michael is waiting for Rudolf to attack him.

C ☐ If the King is killed, then Rudolf Rassendyll will be King forever.

2 Why does the girl at the inn shriek?

A ☐ She knows that Rudolf is not the real King.

B ☐ She recognises Rudolf, but thinks he is the real King.

C ☐ She is frightened of him.

3 Why does Rudolf get so angry with Rupert?

A ☐ Because Rupert offers him money.

B ☐ Because Rupert laughs at him.

C ☐ Because Rupert insults the Princess.

4 Why is Johann pleased to be captured by Rudolf's men?

A ☐ He thinks Michael will kill him when the story is over.

B ☐ He wants to meet the man who is pretending to be the King.

C ☐ He agrees with Michael's plan.

5 What will happen to the King's body when he is killed?

A ☐ It will be thrown into the moat through the window.

B ☐ It will be taken to heaven.

C ☐ It will be thrown down a large pipe into the moat.

6 Why does Rupert call the pipe 'Jacob's Ladder'?

A ☐ He likes being cruel to people.

B ☐ It was built by someone called Jacob.

C ☐ He is very religious.

Comprehension

2 Use what you have learnt in Chapter 5 to draw a simple plan of the castle. Use the words in the box below to help you.

> drawbridge • moat • old part of castle • pipe • stone steps • the King • the Six • two rooms • window

Writing

3 Imagine you are the older Johann looking back on your life. Describe what it was like being in the Castle of Zenda. Who was there? What was happening to the King? How did you feel?

_____

_____

PRE-READING ACTIVITIES

Speaking

4 Read the following statements. What do you think is going to happen in the next chapter? Afterwards, check to see if you were right. Did anything surprise you?

- ☐ I swam over to the castle walls.
- ☐ At that moment, he opened his eyes. He looked terrified.
- ☐ I hid behind Jacob's Ladder.
- ☐ Everyone began firing their guns.
- ☐ I am embarrassed to say I ran away.
- ☐ We rode off down the hill with heavy hearts.

Chapter Six

We Try to Rescue the King

5 The good people of Ruritania would have been very surprised to hear what Johann had told us!

In order to give myself more time to help the King, I made the official reports say I had been seriously injured in a hunting accident. The news caused a lot of public excitement, but Flavia was also very worried. She decided to come to the chateau at Zenda where I was staying, and Marshal Strakencz could do nothing to stop her.

Johann also told us that, although my brother Michael knew I had been injured by Rupert Hentzau, he really believed that my life was in danger. We had to trust Johann, and he seemed to be telling the truth, so we sent him back to Michael the next morning. When Johann arrived at the castle, he was violently punished by Rupert Hentzau for staying out all night with a woman, or so Rupert thought. Michael had approved of this punishment. This made Johann even more angry towards Michael, and more loyal to me.

Flavia was very relieved to find out that I was not as badly injured as she had believed. Even now, when I think of her joy when she saw that I was up and well, and not about to die, my eyes fill with tears. We spent two, happy days together, but our time couldn't last.

We learned from Johann that the King's health was in serious danger, down in that dark prison. He thought the King might not survive much longer. I also had personal reasons for wanting to act soon. I now loved Flavia so much that my life was getting impossibly difficult. Sometimes, I was so desperate to escape this terrible situation, I thought I might run away, but of course I didn't. That wouldn't have helped the King.

Ruritania looked so peaceful. It was perhaps the strangest thing in the history of a country that the King's brother, and a man pretending to be the King, were fighting a secret war for the life of the real King!

❖❖❖

It was very windy and dark the next night. I took Flavia to her rooms. I kissed her hand and said goodnight, then I went straight back to my own rooms, changed and went out. Fritz and Sapt were waiting for me with six men and the horses. We went round the outside of the town, so that no one would see us, and after an hour we started riding up the hill until we arrived at a wood close to Michael's castle. We told the six men to hide there until they were called by Sapt. We saw no one, and hoped Michael still believed I was too badly injured to try to do anything to help the King.

Sapt, Fritz and I carried on until we reached as far as the moat where it passes under the road near the old part of the castle. There was a tree on the edge of the moat. Sapt had brought a long rope with him, which he tied to the tree. I took off my boots, checked that I had my knife in my belt, and lowered myself into the water using the rope. Though the night was wild, the day had been warm and bright, and the water was not cold. I swam over to the castle walls. There were lights on in the new part of the castle, and I heard laughter and shouts. As I got closer, I could see the pipe Johann had called Jacob's Ladder. It was huge, the size of two men together. I was about to swim over to it, when I suddenly saw something, and my heart stopped. By the pipe was a boat, and I could see the shape of a man in it. I went closer and heard the man breathing heavily. I saw that he had a gun next to him, but I was in luck, he was asleep. I pulled my knife out. Of everything I've done in my life, I hate to think about what I did next. It was a terrible thing to attack a man when he was sleeping, but I was trying to save the life of the King. I had no other choice. I raised my hand. At that moment, he opened his eyes. He looked terrified, but I didn't wait. I stabbed[1] him with my knife and killed him. I went straight over to Jacob's Ladder. I could hear a harsh voice in the room above – it was Detchard.

'If you've finished your meal, I need to attach your chains again.'

Next, I heard the King's voice, but I could hardly recognise it. It was so weak and without hope. 'Tell my brother to kill me now. What's he waiting for? I am getting weaker by the day.'

'Your brother doesn't want you dead *yet*,' Detchard answered cruelly.

I heard the door being locked. And then I heard the sobs[2] of the King. He didn't think there was anyone near who could hear him. I wanted to tell the poor King that I was there, but I didn't dare. He would certainly have called out in surprise, and then I would have been discovered. There was nothing more I could do. I went back to the boat, climbed in, and took it back with the dead man to the tree where we had attached the rope. I didn't want anyone to discover his body. The wind was blowing so strongly now, no one would hear what we were doing. When I got back to the tree, I tied the body to the rope, and Sapt and Fritz pulled it up. I told Sapt to call our men. Sapt and Fritz had just pulled the body to the top of the moat, when three men on

---

1. stabbed: 插進 **2. sobs:** 啜泣

horses came out from the castle. At that moment, our six men started galloping towards us, and everyone began firing their guns. I climbed up the rope, and ran over to them. Suddenly, one of the three horses from the castle came galloping towards me. I saw that it was Rupert.

'Oh, it's the idiot King,' he shouted, bringing his sword down on me. I quickly moved out of the way, and avoided being killed by a centimetre. Then, I am embarrassed to say, I ran for my life. My men were coming after him now, shooting at him. Rupert rode as fast as the devil to the moat, and jumped in. I saw him reach the corner of the castle, and then he disappeared.

'Who did we get?' I asked, when Fritz and Sapt arrived.

My men had killed Lauengram and Krafstein, two of the Six. We threw their bodies, and the man I'd killed, into the moat. Then we rode off down the hill with heavy hearts. They'd lost two of their Six, but three of our brave friends were also dead. We were deeply saddened by their deaths, and terribly worried about the King. We were also angry that Rupert Hentzau had beaten us once again, and I hated the fact that I had killed a man in his sleep.

Michael and I had kept our fight a secret until now, but what happened that night at the castle attracted a lot of attention. We had to tell the families of our three men that they'd been killed, but we made it seem as though it had been the result of an argument between a group of friends.

I sent a public apology to Michael, and he sent me an apology back. At least we both agreed not to let the public know what was really going on. In the end, even though we hated each other, we didn't want everyone to find out what was happening, so we kept it all a secret between us.

Through all of this, we were terribly worried about the King, we couldn't try to rescue him again soon.

Because Michael and I were keeping our fight a secret, it was safe for all of us to go to the town of Zenda during the day. In fact, it was rather a ridiculous, even embarrassing, situation.

One day Flavia, Sapt and I were riding in the town, when we saw the head of the Strelsau police.

'I'm here to help the British Ambassador with a mystery,' he explained.

'What mystery is that?' I asked, trying not to sound too interested.

'A young man from his country has gone missing. His friends have not heard from him for two months, and we believe he was last seen in Zenda. A friend of his in Paris, a Mr Featherly, gave us some information, and the men at Zenda station remember seeing his name on some bags.'

'What was the name?'

'Rassendyll, Your Majesty,' he answered. 'The truth is,' he looked over to Flavia, then said in a whisper, 'We think he may have followed a lady here. Do you know Madame de Mauban? We believe she arrived in Ruritania at about the same time as this Rassendyll.'

'Sapt,' I said, 'I must speak a few words in private to the head of police. Will you ride on a short distance with the Princess?'

'This is a very serious matter,' I said, when they'd gone, 'I want you to go back to Strelsau and tell the Ambassador you found some clues[1], but that you need another week. In the meantime, I will try to find out what might have happened to this English man.'

The head of police did not look convinced, but eventually he agreed, and left. I had to stop anyone finding out about Rudolf Rassendyll for a week or even two. This clever man had come close to the truth, and I was angry with George Featherly for gossiping again!

I rode on to catch up with Flavia and Sapt. We reached the far side

1. clues: 線索

of the town, where the road rises to the castle. We looked up and saw a group of riders. As they got closer, we saw that they were travelling with a wooden coffin[1]. Behind it rode a man in black clothes holding his hat in his hand – it was Rupert Hentzau.

Rupert came up to us with a look of great sadness on his face. 'We're taking the body of my friend, Albert of Lauengram,' he said.

'No one could be more upset about these tragic events than me,' I answered looking at the coffin.

'I thank you for your kind words,' said Rupert, but he was looking at Flavia with a smile, and I knew exactly what that evil man was thinking. 'But,' he continued, 'I think others will die before this is over.'

'No one can escape death,' I agreed.

'Yes, even kings die sooner or later,' he said, giving Flavia his most charming smile. Then he rode off and I decided to follow him.

'You fought bravely the other night,' I said. 'You're young, if you can deliver your prisoner to me alive, you won't be harmed.'

He smiled arrogantly and rode closer. 'I have a different idea,' he said in a whisper. 'Attack the castle and I'll help you. We can arrange the right time. Your men might die, but so will Black Michael.'

'What?' I said. I couldn't believe what I was hearing, 'Would you turn against the Duke?'

'Black Michael will fall, like the dog he is,' said Rupert, 'The prisoner, as you call him, will go by Jacob's Ladder. Then only two men will be left, I, Rupert Hentzau, and you, the King of Ruritania.'

'I've never met anyone more evil than you,' I said, shocked at what I was hearing. 'You would make the devil proud.'

'Well, think about it,' and looking over at Flavia. 'She's rather lovely, isn't she?'

I should have hit him for being so rude, but his behaviour was so

---

1. coffin: 棺材

astonishing that it made me laugh. 'Would you really turn against the Duke?' I asked him again.

'He gets in my way. He's such a jealous dog. He made me so angry last night, that I nearly stuck a knife in him!'

'Anything to do with a lady?' I asked.

'Yes, and she's a real beauty, but I think you know her.'

I knew he meant Antoinette de Mauban.

'Your problem is that she prefers the Duke, doesn't she?' I said.

'Yes, and I can't understand why. Well, think about my plan,' he said again. He waved goodbye, and rode off to catch up with the body of his old friend Lauengram. I've met many bad men, but I've never met anyone as difficult to understand as Rupert Hentzau.

'He's very handsome, isn't he?' said Flavia when I returned.

Only on the outside, I thought crossly[1]. I was annoyed with her, perhaps a little jealous.

'What's the matter, Rudolf?' she asked, full of concern.

How could I remain cross when she looked at me like that?

When we got back to the chateau, a servant handed me a letter from Antoinette de Mauban.

Johann carries this for me. I warned you once. In the name of God, and if you are a man, rescue me from these murderers.

I showed the letter to Sapt. 'No one made her go there. She only has herself to blame,' he said, heartlessly.

I knew he was right, but I still felt sorry for Antoinette de Mauban. ■

1. crossly: 生氣地

Reading Comprehension

1 **Are the following statements True or False?**

		T	F
1	Rudolf is fighting for his life.	☐	☐
2	Flavia cries when she sees how ill Rudolf is.	☐	☐
3	Johann thinks that the King won't live for long.	☐	☐
4	Rudolf decides to run away.	☐	☐
5	Nine men ride to the Castle of Zenda to rescue the King.	☐	☐
6	The man in the boat doesn't wake up.	☐	☐
7	Rudolf is proud of everything he did that night.	☐	☐
8	The dead man's body is taken by three men on horses.	☐	☐
9	Rupert tries to kill Rudolf again.	☐	☐
10	By the end of the evening, there are three bodies in the moat.	☐	☐
11	The head of Strelsau police comes to Zenda, looking for a British man.	☐	☐
12	Rupert tells Rudolf he is happy to betray Michael.	☐	☐

Writing Summaries

2 **Write a short police report about the failed rescue of the King. Remember to only include the facts!**

_____

_____

_____

_____

_____

_____

_____

_____

_____

Grammar

3a **Fill in the gaps below with the correct form of the verb in brackets. Use either the past simple or the past perfect.**

My men told me they (**1**) _____ (kill) Lauengram and Krafstein, two of the Six. We (**2**) _____ (throw) their dead bodies, and that of the man I (**3**) _____ (kill), into the moat. Then we (**4**) _____ (ride) off down the hill with heavy hearts. They (**5**) _____ (lose) two of their Six, but three of our brave friends (**6**) _____ (be) also dead. We (**7**) _____ (be) terribly sad that they (**8**) _____ (die), and we were terribly worried about the King. We (**9**) _____ (be) also angry that Rupert Hentzau (**10**) _____ (manage) to escape us once again.

3b **What do you notice about the past simple and the past perfect?**

Speaking

4 **What did you think of this chapter? Did you find it exciting? Was it difficult to follow all the action? Did anything surprise or shock you?**

PRE-READING ACTIVITIES

Listening

▶ 6 **5** **Relationships get complicated in the next chapter. Read the following statements and decide if they are correct. Then listen to the next chapter and find out if you were right.**

1 Flavia loves Rudolf, but she doesn't love Michael. ☐
2 Rudolf must pretend to love Flavia. ☐
3 Michael loves Flavia, but he doesn't really love Antoinette. ☐
4 Antoinette loves Michael, but she doesn't like Rupert Hentzau. ☐
5 Rupert wants Antoinette, and he finds Flavia attractive. ☐
6 Everyone hates Michael! ☐

A Desperate Plan

▶ 6 Because I'd gone out in public into the town of Zenda, I could no longer pretend to be badly injured. Indeed, after that, the atmosphere changed in the town. There were more soldiers about, and Black Michael's castle was being carefully guarded. I wanted to help Madame de Mauban, but didn't see how I could. I was as powerless to help her as I had been to help the King.

In Strelsau, people were beginning to talk about how long I was staying away from the capital. For now, they forgave me because Flavia was with me; they thought the two love birds wanted to spend time together, but they wouldn't let me stay away forever.

My politicians regularly came from Strelsau to visit me at the chateau. One day, when Flavia and I were sitting together, Strakencz and the Chancellor made me promise I would become publicly engaged to Flavia. In Ruritania, a public engagement is as important as the marriage itself. What could I say? We agreed a date for a ceremony at the cathedral in two weeks' time.

Everyone celebrated at this news. There were only two men in the whole kingdom who didn't. The first was Michael, and the second was me – I knew I could never really marry her; and there was only one man in the whole kingdom who knew nothing about it – the true King of Ruritania.

❖ ❖ ❖

Three days later, Johann came to see us in secret, greedy for more money. Johann had been with the Duke when he'd been told of my engagement to Flavia. The Duke's face had gone black with anger. He became even angrier when Rupert said he thought that by capturing his brother, the Duke had given Ruritania a better king than they'd had for years, *and* given the Princess a better husband. Michael had shouted at him to leave after that!

There was bad news however. The King was very sick: Johann had seen him, and he had wasted away[1] and was hardly able to move. The Duke was worried enough to get a doctor from Strelsau. The doctor went to see the King, and when he came out of the cell, he was pale and trembling. The doctor begged[2] the Duke to let him go back to Strelsau, but the Duke refused. The doctor was now a prisoner of the Duke, who told him his life was safe if the King lived, and for as long as the Duke decided he could live. The doctor did persuade them to let Madame de Mauban help him look after the King. So, the King was dying while I walked around free and in good health. This made everyone at the Castle of Zenda depressed. They hardly spoke to each other, except to argue, which was very often.

I promised Johann a lot of money if he would go back to the castle for one more night. I asked him to tell Madame de Mauban I was trying to help her, and, if she could, speak one word of comfort to the King.

'How is the King guarded now that two of the Six are dead?' I asked.

'Detchard and Bersonin watch at night, Rupert Hentzau and De Gautet during the day. There are a few soldiers in a room above, but the door to the room where they are guarding the King is locked, and only the four have a key.'

---

1. **wasted away:** 因病消瘦

2. **begged:** 乞求

'Where are the Duke's rooms?' I asked Johann.

'In the modern part of the castle, on the first floor. His rooms are on the right as you go towards the drawbridge. Madame de Mauban's rooms are opposite his, but her door is locked at night after she has entered it.'

'To keep her safe from Rupert Hentzau, I suppose.'

'Perhaps,' said Johann. 'The drawbridge is pulled up at night. The Duke is the only one with the key to that. I sleep with five servants in the entrance hall in the modern part of the castle. The servants don't have guns.'

I made a plan there and then. I'd failed at Jacob's Ladder the first time, I would fail again there. I must make the attack from the other side.

'Now, Johann, at exactly two o'clock in the morning, you must open the main entrance to the castle.'

'And may I escape by the door, sir, when I have opened it?'

'Yes, go as quick as your legs will carry you. One thing more. Carry this note to Madame. Tell her if she cares for any of our lives, she must do what I have asked her in the note.'

Johann was trembling[1] with fear, but time was running out, we had no other choice. When Johann had gone, I called Fritz and Sapt, and told them my plan.

'You must stay here and take care of the Princess,' said Fritz.

'Yes,' agreed Sapt, 'If you and the King are both killed, we'll have lost everything.'

'No, if we're both killed, then you'll serve your new queen, Flavia.'

There was a pause. Then Sapt said, so seriously that both Fritz and I burst out laughing, 'I wish King Rudolf the Third had married your ancestor!'

'Come,' said I, 'It is the King we are thinking about. If the real King isn't free before Flavia and I are engaged, then I will have to tell Flavia the truth.' Sapt and Fritz looked at me, but didn't argue any more.

---

1. trembling: 顫抖

❖ ❖ ❖

Here's the plan I made. Sapt would take a group of soldiers up to the door of the modern part of the castle. They were to kill anyone who saw them, but only using swords. I didn't want any noisy gun shots going off at this time. If all went well, then they would be at the door when Johann opened it. They were to rush in and attack the five servants. At the same moment, Madame de Mauban was to scream "Help! Michael help! Rupert Hentzau!" She would pretend that she was being attacked by Rupert.

At this point, we hoped Michael would come running out of his rooms, and there he would meet Sapt and his men. They would capture the Duke and let down the drawbridge. Hearing his name, Rupert, who slept in the old part of the castle, would come across the bridge; De Gautet might or might not come with him. And when Rupert stepped onto the drawbridge? This was my part of the plan. I would swim across the moat and hide under the drawbridge. I would then climb up onto it, and kill Rupert and De Gautet if he was there.

That would leave only Bersonin and Detchard guarding the King. We would take the keys from Rupert and De Gautet, and open the door. At this point, we would have to move quickly to stop them killing the King and putting his body down Jacob's Ladder into the moat.

I gave orders that our chateau was to be lit as if there was a large party. Marshal Strakencz would be there. If we hadn't returned by morning, he was to go to the castle and demand to see the King. If the King was dead, then he must take Flavia immediately back to Strelsau, and make her queen. To be honest, this is what I thought most likely to happen. In truth, I didn't believe I, or the King, or Michael had much more than a day to live.

I went to say goodnight to the Princess. She looked quiet and subdued[1], but as I was about to leave, she put her arms round me. Then, looking shy, she put a ring on my finger. I was wearing the King's ring, but I also had a Rassendyll family ring on my little finger. I took this off and put it on her finger. 'Wear that ring, even though you will wear another ring when you are queen,' I said.

'Whatever happens,' she said, 'I will wear it until I die.'

The night was fine and clear. I'd prayed for bad weather like we'd had during the last attack, but luck was against us. At twelve o'clock, Sapt and his men left the chateau, and went on a back road to the Castle of Zenda. They planned to arrive in front of the castle at a quarter to two. Hiding their horses nearby, they would then go on foot towards the entrance and make themselves ready for when Johann opened the door at two, as we'd arranged. If the door didn't open at two, then they must send Fritz round the other side of the castle to meet me. If I was not there, they must gallop back to the chateau where we'd been staying, get Marshal Strakencz and his soldiers, and return immediately to the Castle of Zenda. If I was not there to meet Fritz, then they could be certain I was dead, and if I was dead, five minutes later the King would be dead too.

We must now leave Sapt and his friends, and I will tell you what happened to me during this night of adventure. I left on a good horse, taking my sword. I was wearing clothes that would keep me as warm as possible, but that I could still move in. Although the water in the moat was not cold, I would be in it a long time, and I was worried that the cold would take all my energy and courage.

I hid my horse and moved silently up to the castle. I tied a rope around me, attached it to the same tree that we had found the first time we'd tried to rescue the King. I lowered myself into the moat

---

1. **subdued:** 若有所思、憂心

and swam over to my old friend, Jacob's Ladder. Then, I hid behind the great pipe, and waited.

The drawbridge was still open. I could see a window on the right of the bridge, that must be the Duke's room, on the other side was Madame de Mauban's room. I prayed that she wouldn't forget her part in the plan. Suddenly, someone opened the Duke's window wide, and I saw Antoinette de Mauban. A moment later, a man came up to her and tried to put his arm around her, but she moved away from him. I heard a laugh that I recognised. It was Rupert. His head was close to hers. I suppose he whispered to her, for I saw her point to the moat, and I heard her say, in slow, distinct tones, 'I would rather throw myself out of this window.'

'I can't understand why you're so in love with Black Michael,' he said, impatiently, 'He doesn't care about you. He is mad about the Princess, and all he talks about is cutting that other idiot's throat.'

He was talking about me of course! If I hadn't left my gun with my horse, I'd have shot him there and then. I heard the noise of a door opening. A man's angry voice said, 'What are you doing here?'

'I was apologising to her that you were not here, I could hardly leave her alone,' Rupert replied, rudely.

I saw Black Michael come towards Rupert and take his arm. 'There's room for more than one body in the moat,' he said.

'Are you threatening me?' asked Rupert.

'A threat is more warning than most people get from me,' the Duke said, 'Now, let's change the subject. Are Detchard and Bersonin guarding our prisoner? Then, go back across the drawbridge, unless you want to swim to your bed, I will be raising it in ten minutes.'

Rupert left. The window was shut and I could see or hear no more. Then I heard Rupert on the drawbridge calling De Gautet.

They walked across the bridge arm in arm. Rupert stopped in the middle of the bridge, and leant over the wall. He was standing right above where I was. I immediately hid behind Jacob's Ladder. He took a bottle from De Gautet. He finished what was in it, and threw it into the moat – it fell very close to the pipe. Then he started shooting at it. The first two shots missed the bottle but hit the pipe, the third hit the bottle. He fired several times at the pipe and I felt one of the bullets whistle past me! Then, to my relief, a voice cried, 'Bridge closing!' and Rupert and De Gautet ran across. The bridge was raised, and the clock rang out, it was only quarter past one.

Some ten minutes later, I saw Rupert come out of the old castle door again with a sword in his hand. He climbed down some steps in the old wall that I hadn't noticed until now. When he reached the bottom, he climbed into the water and swam across to the new part of the castle, with his sword between his teeth. When he reached the other side, he climbed up some more hidden steps, took a key from his pocket, unlocked a door, and disappeared.

I swam over to the old side of the castle and climbed halfway up the steps Rupert had just climbed down. I waited, sword in hand, until the clock rang half past one. The Duke's room was dark. There was a light on in the window of Madame de Mauban's room, but nothing moved.

So, mine wasn't the only secret plan in the castle that night. What *was* Rupert doing?

Reading Comprehension

1a Rudolf's plan is clever, but quite complicated. Answer the following questions to make sure you understand what is happening. Remember, the King's life depends on everyone getting this right!

1 What does Rudolf ask Johann to do and at what time?

_____

2 What *two* things does Rudolf want to happen after Johann has opened the door?

_____

_____

3 What does Rudolf say will happen to Michael then?

_____

4 What will happen to Rupert (and perhaps also to De Gautet)?

_____

5 What does Rudolf say Strakencz must do if Rudolf and his men do not return to the chateau?

_____

6 What does Rudolf do first on this 'night of adventure'?

_____

_____

7 It's quarter past one, what has just happened?

_____

_____

8 It's half past one, describe what has just happened.

_____

_____

1b Can you see any weaknesses in Rudolf's plan? What do you think might go wrong?

Reading for First

2 **Fill in the gaps in the text below with the correct sentence A-D.**

A He finished what was in it, and threw it into the moat.

B They walked across the bridge arm in arm.

C The bridge was raised, and the clock rang out, it was only quarter past one.

D I immediately hid behind Jacob's Ladder.

Rupert left. The window was shut and I could see or hear no more. Then I heard Rupert on the drawbridge calling De Gautet. **1** ☐ Rupert stopped in the middle of the bridge, and leant over the wall. He was standing right above where I was. **2** ☐ He took a bottle from De Gautet. **3** ☐ It fell very close to the pipe. Then he started shooting at it. The first two shots missed the bottle but hit the pipe, the third hit the bottle. He fired several times at the pipe and I felt one of the bullets whistle past me! Then, to my relief, a voice cried, 'Bridge closing!' and Rupert and De Gautet ran across. **4** ☐

PRE-READING ACTIVITIES

Listening

▶ 7 **3** **As you listen to the first part of Chapter 8, write down the name of the person who says the following.**

1 'Help! Help! Michael help!' _____

2 'Open the door!' _____

3 'What's the matter?' _____

4 'That's for you, Johann!' _____

5 'Help!' _____

Chapter Eight

Rupert Hentzau!

▶ 7 You might think that at this point I didn't have time to stand and think, but for the next moment or two I thought about the situation deeply. At least Rupert Hentzau was on the other side of the bridge from the King. That left only three men for me to deal with – De Gautet in his bed, and the other two guarding the King, Bersonin and Detchard. Oh, if only I had the key, I could have opened the door and gone to attack them!

I waited for what seemed like half an hour, but was probably only five minutes. All was quiet in the modern part of the castle. Then there was a very faint sound, like a key opening a door. I soon found out what it was, because the next moment, there was a crash from Madame de Mauban's room. It sounded as though glass had been broken. The window suddenly went dark, then a woman cried out, 'Help! Help! Michael help!' followed by a terrified scream.

I was still over by the old part of the castle, I climbed up to the top step and suddenly, I saw a dark corner on the other side of the drawbridge where I could hide unseen. I ran across and hid there in total silence. In this way, no man could go between the old and new parts of the castle without meeting me, and my sword, first. There was another scream, a door was opened violently, and smashed[1] against the wall.

I heard the voice of Black Michael. 'Open the door!' he shouted. I

1. smashed: 撞擊

could hear him trying to open Madame de Mauban's door. 'In God's name, what's the matter?'

He was answered by the exact words I had asked her to say in my note, 'Help, Michael – Rupert Hentzau!'

The Duke shouted and threw himself against Madame de Mauban's door again. At the same moment, I heard a window open above my head, and someone shouted, 'What's the matter?'

I grasped[1] my sword – if De Gautet got near me, then one more of the Six would soon be dead. After that, everything seemed to happen at once. There was an angry cry from Madame's room, followed by the cry of a wounded man; the window was flung[2] open; young Rupert stood there sword in hand. He turned his back and I saw his body go forward.

'That's for you, Johann!' he cried, raising his sword.

So Johann was there too, come to help the Duke. If he was injured, then who would open the castle gate for Sapt and his men?

The Duke called out in a weak voice, 'Help!'

I saw that Rupert was now fighting five or six men. He defended himself well and jumped up on to the window. Then, laughing wildly[3] and waving his sword, he jumped head first into the moat. I didn't see what happened to him next, because as he jumped, De Gautet's thin face looked out of the door next to where I was hiding. Without a second's hesitation, I struck him with my sword, and he fell dead in the doorway without a sound. I searched his body desperately for the key. In my panic, I spoke to him as if he were still alive, 'Where's the key man, where's the key?' Eventually, I found it. I opened the door to the room where Bersonin and Detchard were guarding the King. I relocked it, and put the key in my pocket. I was at the top of some narrow stone stairs.

'What the devil's happening?' It was Detchard.

'Shall we kill the King?' asked another voice.

---

1. **grasped:** 緊抓
2. **flung:** 打開

3. **wildly:** 瘋狂地

I nearly sobbed with relief when I heard Detchard say, 'No, wait, there'll be trouble if we kill him too soon.'

I heard the door begin to open at the bottom of the stairs. At that moment, I rushed down the stairs and ran straight in through the door. Bersonin was astonished to see me and almost fell backwards. I pushed him against the wall with my sword, and in an instant he lay dead on the floor. I turned, but Detchard was no longer there. He'd run straight to the King's room, shutting the door behind him. I am sure that he would have killed the King, and perhaps me too, if a wonderful and brave man hadn't died to save the King. I forced open the door and saw the King in a corner of the room, in chains. Broken by his sickness, he could do nothing. He had chains around his wrists and was moving his arms up and down uselessly, laughing like a madman. Detchard and the doctor were together in the middle of the room; the doctor had thrown himself on the murderer. At the exact moment when I entered the room, Detchard broke free of the doctor and stabbed him with his sword. The poor doctor fell down dead at his feet. Then Detchard turned to me and shouted, 'At last!'

We fought sword to sword. I can remember very little of it now, except that he was an excellent swordsman, better than me. He pushed me back towards Jacob's Ladder. I saw a smile on his face and then he wounded[1] me in my left arm.

I didn't win that fight by myself. I believe Detchard would have killed me, and murdered the King, for he was the most skilful swordsman I have ever met. But even as he was close to beating me in the fight, the half-mad man that had once been Prince Rudolf, jumped about shrieking and laughing, 'It's my cousin Rudolf! Cousin Rudolf! I'll help you, cousin Rudolf!' he shrieked, picking himself up and coming towards us.

---

1. **wounded**: 弄傷

I became filled with hope once more. 'Push the chair into his legs!' I shouted. Detchard attacked me again and almost killed me. 'Come on! Come on, man!' I cried, 'Come and share the fun!'

The King pushed the chair in front of him. Detchard turned then, and before I knew what he was doing, had turned his sword on the King. With a terrible cry, the King fell to the floor. Detchard turned back to me, but his actions had prepared his own death, because as he turned, he stepped into the blood flowing from the doctor's body. He slipped and fell. In that instant, I raised my sword, and pushed the point through his neck. He lay dead across the body of the doctor.

Was the King dead? I rushed[1] over to him. It seemed as if he was dead. He had a great cut across his head and he was lying on the floor without moving. I knelt down to see if he was still breathing, but before I could hear anything, there was a loud noise – the drawbridge was being lowered! I was in a trap and the King with me. I went back into the first room, and took Bersonin's gun. My arm was bleeding heavily, so I quickly tore off a piece of my shirt and wrapped the material round my arm. I'd run out of energy, I felt exhausted.

I went up the steps to the door onto the bridge, then I heard the laugh I knew so well. It was Rupert Hentzau! That laugh told me my men had *not* come. I heard the clock strike half past two! My God! That meant that Johann hadn't opened the castle door! Fritz would have gone round to the other side of the castle to meet me, but I wasn't there! If that happened, I had told my men to go back to the chateau to tell everyone that the King and I were dead. I was alone with my enemies. If the King and I weren't dead yet, we soon would be. I was sure that Rupert was coming to get me, but then Rupert said something I wasn't expecting, 'Come and fight me on the bridge, you dogs! Tell Black Michael to come and fight me himself!'

---

1. rushed: 衝

So, he hadn't come to fight *me* at all! I saw that I might now have a chance to win. I turned the key in the door and looked out. At the other end of the bridge stood three or four terrified men. They didn't have any guns to defend themselves with, only long sticks. They were staring at a man standing in the centre of the bridge, sword in hand. It was Rupert Hentzau of course. His clothes were covered in blood, but he didn't look injured himself. Behind the men, I saw my friend Johann. He had blood running down his cheek.

I could have shot Rupert then, but I decided not to! My sense of honour wouldn't let me shoot this young man in the back. So I did nothing.

'Michael, you dog! Michael! If you can stand, come on!' he shouted again.

In answer to his shouts, I heard the desperate shout of a woman. 'He's dead! My God, the Duke's dead!'

'Dead?' shouted Rupert, 'Then I did better than I thought!' And he laughed at this news of his victory. Suddenly, I heard noises from outside the castle, though no one else seemed to pay any attention to them, their attention was held by what was happening before their eyes on the drawbridge. Those noises meant that my men hadn't gone back to Zenda! My heart was filled with hope.

'Put your sticks down, men,' Rupert said, 'Now that Michael is dead, you will do what I tell you.'

They were about to do what he said, when Madame de Mauban suddenly appeared. She walked through the group of men and out onto the bridge. Her eyes shone wildly and in her shaking hand she held a gun. She fired it at Rupert Hentzau, but missed. Rupert laughed at her, but Antoinette de Mauban took no notice. With a wonderful effort, she calmed herself and she began to raise her arm

again. Before she could shoot, he smiled politely and called out, 'Well, I could never kill a woman I am in love with,' and before any of us could stop him, he jumped once again into the moat. Then I heard a voice I knew. It was Sapt.

'God! It's the Duke, dead!'

I knew that the King was safe now. I dropped my gun and jumped onto the bridge. There was a cry of surprise from the men. 'The King!' they shouted, and then I, like Rupert Hentzau, jumped off the bridge, with my sword in my hand. My only thought was to kill that evil man, Rupert Hentzau. The only problem was that Rupert was swimming away quickly, and my arm was badly injured, but I was determined to reach him. Rupert found the rope I'd left earlier, and began to climb up out of the moat. Then he saw me swimming towards him. I think he thought I was the King. Then he realised who it was. 'Oh, it's the *idiot* king again!' he said. When he got to the top, he waved at me. 'I would love to stay and talk, but things are a bit too hot for me here!' he said, and disappeared. Without thinking of the danger, I climbed up the rope after him. He was thirty metres in front of me, and running very fast. I ran after him, hungry for his blood and soon we were deep in the dark forest of Zenda. It was three o'clock in the morning and just beginning to get light. He turned and waved at me, mocking[1] me because I'd stopped to get my breath back. A moment later, he turned right and I could no longer see him. I thought I'd lost him, when I heard a girl scream. I ran towards the sound, and saw Rupert lifting a young girl gently off her horse. She screamed again, then he kissed her, and got onto the horse. I'd nearly reached him.

'What did you do in the castle?' he called out to me.

'I killed three of your friends,' I said, breathlessly.

1. **mocking:** 嘲笑

'What? You got there? And what about the King?'

'He was injured by Detchard, but I hope that he's still alive,' then I said to him, 'I didn't kill you on the bridge just now, Rupert Hentzau, when I had the chance! Get off your horse and fight like a man!'

'In front of a young lady? You surprise me, Your Majesty!' he said, looking at the girl he'd just lifted from her horse. When I heard that, I became so angry I hardly knew what I was doing. I ran at him with my sword and cut his cheek open. He sat without moving and I think was stunned[1] by my attack. I was exhausted now and fell down to my knees. I could do no more, and he would have killed me then I am sure, except at that moment there was a shout behind me. I turned and saw a man riding full speed towards us, with a gun in his hand. It was Fritz von Tarlenheim, my faithful[2] friend. At that point, Rupert knew he had better leave, but before he went, he pushed his hair off his forehead. Leaning forward, he smiled and said, 'Goodbye, Rudolf Rassendyll!'

Fritz fired his gun at him, but by some miracle, he missed. Rupert didn't wait to receive another shot, and rode away as fast as he could with the blood pouring from the wound in his cheek. I shouted at Fritz to ride after him, but instead, he got off his horse and came towards me, and that devil of a man escaped from us again!

'Fritz!' I said.

'Yes, my friend, my dear friend!' he answered.

'Is the King alive?' I asked.

He kissed me on the forehead, 'Yes, he is alive,' he said, 'Thanks to the bravest man I know, the King is alive!'

The young girl stood nearby weeping[3] with fright. She was staring at me, thinking I was the King. I was in too much pain to speak. I laid my head in Fritz's arms, shut my eyes and went to sleep.

---

1. stunned: 呆若木雞
2. faithful: 忠誠

3. weeping: 哭

Reading Comprehension

1a Anthony Hope includes a wide variety of sounds in his description of the events in this chapter. This helps the story become more dramatic. Match each sound (1-10), with a phrase from the box below.

> door opened violently • Duke called out • glass broken • injured man • key opening a door • "Open the door!" • Rudolf hid on the bridge • Rudolf waited • swords • terrified woman

1 quiet in modern part of castle _____

2 faint sound _____

3 crash _____

4 scream _____

5 total silence _____

6 smashed against a wall _____

7 shout _____

8 hitting each other _____

9 cry _____

10 weak voice _____

1b Using your answers from 1a, write a short summary of the events in this chapter up to the moment when Michael is injured.

2 In this chapter, who... (Use the names on the left to help you.)

Who...	gets killed (and by who)	gets injured (by who)	tries to kill Rupert
Antoinette de Mauban			
Johann			
Black Michael			
De Gautet			
Bersonin			
the doctor			
Rudolf			
Detchard			
the King			
Rupert Hentzau			
Fritz			

Speaking

3a Do you agree or disagree with the following statements?

	Agree	Disagree
1 I feel sorry for Black Michael.	☐	☐
2 Rupert Hentzau is a terrible man.	☐	☐
3 Rudolf Rassendyll is a coward.	☐	☐
4 Antoinette de Mauban has gone mad.	☐	☐
5 Detchard is a brave man.	☐	☐

3b Now discuss your answers. Remember to give reasons for your decision.

PRE-READING ACTIVITIES

Speaking

4 Talk in pairs. What's going to happen next? Tick the statements you agree with, then listen to the last chapter and see if you were right!

1 The King will die, and Sapt will ask Rudolf to be King of Ruritania. ☐

2 Antoinette de Mauban will return to Paris, and marry George Featherly. ☐

3 The people of Ruritania will be told what Rudolf did to save their King. ☐

4 The Princess will never discover the true identity of the man she loves. ☐

5 The Princess will marry the King, and become Queen of Ruritania. ☐

6 Rudolf will return to London, and get a job as a diplomat. ☐

Chapter Nine

If Love was the Only Thing in the World...

In order for you to understand what happened that night, I need to add the stories of Fritz von Tarlenheim and Antoinette de Mauban.

Duke Michael had asked Madame de Mauban to travel from Paris to be with him in Ruritania. It soon became clear that she wasn't the only woman he was interested in. Michael didn't hide his plan to marry Flavia from her, but Antoinette was too much in love with him to leave him. Love didn't rule her completely though – she didn't want me to be killed, and she certainly didn't want the Duke to marry Flavia. This was why she decided to help us.

After she'd arrived at the Castle of Zenda, the situation had got more complicated. Rupert had become attracted to her. He was a man who always got what he wanted, but she hated him. Every day, there had been angry scenes between Rupert and Michael. She wasn't surprised when I told her about Rupert's plan to betray the Duke. She said she'd warned him many times about Rupert.

So, on this night, Rupert had been determined to get what he wanted. He had got a key to her room and gone in. Her screams had woken the Duke. The two men had fought, and the Duke had been fatally wounded[1] by Rupert. Antoinette had waited with the Duke until he'd died, then she'd come to the bridge with the intention of

1. **fatally wounded:** 受致命傷

killing Rupert. She hadn't seen me until I jumped into the moat.

At that point, my friends had arrived. They'd arrived in front of the castle entrance at the right time, but Johann had still been fighting to save the Duke, so he couldn't open the door as we'd planned. Sapt, Fritz and the men had waited until half past two, then, instead of going back to the chateau to take Flavia to Strelsau as we'd arranged, they'd decided to break down the door of the castle. It had taken them several minutes, but eventually they'd forced open the door, and gone upstairs where they had found the body of the Duke. Then they'd come to the bridge and when Michael's servants had discovered he was dead, they'd given themselves up immediately. Antoinette told Sapt I'd jumped off the bridge. Sapt and Fritz, with the other men behind them, had crossed the bridge in silence. Fritz had nearly tripped[1] over the body of De Gautet. There hadn't been a sound anywhere.

One of my men went back to Michael's body to get the key to the door. When he returned with it, they'd opened the door and gone down the steps. At the bottom they'd found Bersonin, dead. They'd gone into the King's room, terrified at what they might find. First, they'd seen the body of Detchard lying across the doctor, then they'd seen the King lying on the ground with a terrible cut on his head. Sapt had examined him, and found that he was still alive! They'd removed the King's chains, covered his face so that no one would know who he was and carried him to the Duke's room, where Antoinette had looked after him until a doctor came. At this point, Fritz had jumped on his horse, and gone to look for me in the forest. By chance, he'd heard me shout at Rupert. He'd followed my voice, riding as fast as he could to save me.

As you can imagine, it was not easy to try and keep all of this a secret from the public! Antoinette and Johann promised to say nothing, and Sapt told everyone that the man they'd carried over the bridge was

---

1. **tripped:** 絆倒

a friend of the King. The King had gone to rescue his friend, Sapt told everyone, but he'd been badly hurt, and was now fighting for his life. A message was sent to Marshal Strakencz in Zenda. He was to tell the Princess that the King was safe, and to wait at the chateau. Strakencz was told to bring his men to the Castle of Zenda straight away.

This plan worked well. The whole town of Zenda was talking about how brave the King was, and about what a bad man the Duke had been. Everyone was asking, who was this friend that the King had risked his own life to rescue? Well, I should say that the plan worked well except for one thing. Of course, the Princess didn't stay at the chateau for one minute after she'd heard what had happened. Nothing would stop her from coming to see me.

By this time, Fritz and I had arrived at the edge of the forest. We saw the Princess coming up the hill on her horse, with Strakencz and some of his soldiers. We knew she mustn't see us. We hid behind some trees, but we'd forgotten about the young girl who Rupert had taken the horse from. She'd followed us all the way to the edge of the forest and now she went running up to the Princess.

'Please, Madame, the King is here, hiding behind those trees. Shall I take you to him?'

'That cannot be true,' said Strakencz, trying to keep the Princess away from me. 'The King is in the castle, he's been badly injured.'

'Yes, he is injured,' said the girl, 'but he's over there with his friend.'

'Is he in two places, or are there two kings?' asked Flavia, completely confused. Flavia got off her horse.

'I will go and see this gentleman,' she said.

Sapt arrived next and tried to make the best of a bad situation. Everyone was starting to get suspicious. 'Let me go and look,' Sapt said quickly.

'And I will come with you,' said the princess.

'Then you must come by yourself,' he whispered to her.

When I saw that they were coming, I sat on the ground and hid my face in my hands. I could not look at her. Fritz was next to me, with his hand on my shoulder.

'It's him!' the Princess cried, half afraid, and half happy to find me. 'Are you hurt?' She sat by me, and gently pulled my hands away from my face.

'It is the King!' she said. 'Please explain. I don't understand why you didn't tell me the truth!'

None of us answered her. Then she threw her arms round me and kissed me.

'It is not the King,' Sapt said, quietly, 'Don't kiss him; he's not the King.'

'But it is my love, it is Rudolf. What do you mean?' she said.

'It's not the King,' said Sapt again. Fritz looked terribly upset.

'Look at me, Rudolf! Look at me. What does it mean?' the Princess asked.

Then I looked into her eyes, and said, 'God forgive me, dear Princess, I'm not the King!'

She looked at me in horror. Then with a cry of pain, I pulled her to me and kissed her. I wished then that Rupert had killed me. I couldn't suffer like this!

I spent the day after the fight hiding in the forest. When it got dark, Fritz took me to the castle in secret. I was taken to the cell where they had kept the King. The great pipe they had called Jacob's Ladder had gone. Later, Johann brought me something to eat. He looked pale from his wound, but was not too badly hurt. He told me the King was recovering, that the Princess had seen him, and that she and the King had spent a long time talking to Fritz and Sapt. Fritz came into the cell when I'd finished eating. 'The King wants to see you,' he said, 'Follow me.' We went straight up to the Duke's old rooms.

The King was lying on the Duke's bed. He looked very weak. 'I can't talk to you for long,' he said, 'I wanted to take you to Strelsau and keep you with me, and tell everyone what you had done; and you would have been my best and nearest friend, Cousin Rudolf. But they tell me I must not, and that the secret must be kept – if kept it can be.'

'They are right, Your Majesty. Let me go. My work here is done.'

'You've done what no other man could have done, and you've shown me how to be a good King.' I thought how difficult it had been not to betray him, as I had fallen more and more in love with Flavia! 'I don't know when I'll see you again,' he said, so quietly that I could hardly hear him.

'If you ever need me again…' I said, kissing the King's hand. Then, Fritz took me away. 'The Princess wants to see you,' he said.

'Does she know everything?'

'Yes,' he answered, opening a door. The Princess was standing by the window.

'Flavia!' I said, softly.

She made me sit, knelt at my feet and laid her head against me. I'd come to ask her to forgive me for lying to her, for pretending to be someone I was not, but that wasn't what was worrying her. She was worried that I'd only pretended to love her, as I'd pretended to be the King.

'Oh Flavia, I never pretended to love you. I love you with all my heart!' I said, 'From the moment I saw you in the Cathedral, there has only been one woman in the world for me, and there will be no other for the rest of my life. I am so sorry for what I've done to you.'

'They made you do it,' she said quickly, 'And I don't think it would have changed anything if I had known the truth. I only ever loved you. It was always you, never the King!'

'I nearly told you the truth on the night of the party, but Sapt interrupted me,' I said, 'And several times I nearly left the King to die because I didn't want to lose you!'

'I know! I know! But what are we going to do now, Rudolf?'

I put my arm around her and pulled her up to sit next to me. 'I'm going away tonight.'

'Oh no, not tonight!' cried the Princess.

'I must go tonight, before more people have seen me.' And so we talked and talked about what we could do. I even tried to persuade her to come with me back to England.

'If love was the only thing there was,' she said, eventually, 'then you wouldn't have risked your life to save the King, you would have tried to stay with me. In the same way, I have a duty to Ruritania and to my people. That is why I cannot go with you.'

So, it was over. I stood to go. 'I will always think of you,' I said.

'The bravest and best man I know! Perhaps we'll never see each other again. Kiss me, my dear, and then go, leave!'

I kissed her and, with the greatest difficulty, I left her with tears in her eyes.

I walked away from her and didn't look back. Fritz and Sapt rode with me through the night, until we reached the first train station outside Ruritania. I kept my face covered so that no one would recognise me.

'We've had some adventures together, haven't we old friends?' I said to them, as I was getting on the train.

Fritz politely took off his hat, as he used to when I was King. Then he took my hand and kissed it. 'Heaven doesn't always make the right men kings!' he said.

Even Sapt held my hand and looked upset to see me go. He and Fritz stood at the station until I could no longer see them from the train.

Now, I had to travel back to my old life, where no one would ever know that I had been a king for three months! As I sat on the train, I could still hear Flavia's voice in my head, calling my name. I think you can imagine, dear reader, how I felt at leaving my beautiful Flavia!

The details of my return aren't particularly interesting. I went to the Austrian mountains to rest, but I had a nervous reaction to everything I'd been through, which made me as weak as a baby. I developed a very bad cold and ended up spending a fortnight[1] in bed. I sent a postcard to my brother telling him where I was and when I planned to return. That would stop people worrying about where I was, and keep the head of police in Strelsau happy!

When I got better I travelled to Paris, and went to visit my old friend George Featherly. He'd decided that I'd travelled to Strelsau to be with Madame de Mauban. She'd returned to Paris and now lived a quiet life, but people were still gossiping about what might have happened to her. George wouldn't stop talking until he'd invented a love affair between Madame de Mauban and myself. George was also sure he knew the "truth" about what had happened in Ruritania that summer. In his opinion, there was more to be said about Black Michael than the public realised. 'In fact,' he went on, 'there was a strong suspicion that the Prisoner of Zenda was not a man at all, but a woman disguised as a man.'

'Perhaps that woman was Antoinette de Mauban herself!' I said with a smile, but George told me to stop being ridiculous.

I wrote to Antoinette while I was in Paris. She sent me an

---

1. fortnight: 兩個星期

affectionate[1] reply promising once again that she'd never tell anyone what had really happened in Ruritania.

When I got back to London, my sister-in-law was furious with me. 'We've wasted a lot of time trying to find you,' she said.

'I know you have,' I said, 'you sent half our diplomats looking for me. But why were you so worried? I can take care of myself.'

'Oh, we weren't worried about you,' she said, 'We needed to speak to you because I've found you a job. Sir Jacob Borrodaile, who you know, has been given a new embassy, and he wants you to go with him.'

'Where's he going?'

'He's going to be the new Ambassador of Strelsau,' she said, 'you couldn't have a nicer place!'

'Strelsau?' I said, looking carefully at my brother, 'Oh, I don't think that's a good idea at all.'

'Oh, nobody remembers that old story about your ancestor and the Elphbergs any more,' said Rose.

In my pocket, I had a photograph of the King of Ruritania, taken a month before he became King. 'Here's a picture of Rudolf V,' I said, showing it to them, 'Don't you think they might remember the story if I went there?'

My sister-in-law looked at the photograph, and then at me. 'Good heavens!' she said.

'What do you think, Bob?' I asked my brother.

Instead of answering me, he got up and went to a corner of the room where there was a great pile of newspapers. He came back with a copy of the *Illustrated London News*. He opened up the paper and showed us a large photograph of the coronation of Rudolf V at Strelsau. He put this and my photograph next to each other. I looked

---

1. **affectionate:** 溫馨的

at the newspaper, and saw my own face standing with Sapt, Marshal Strakencz, the Cardinal, Black Michael, and my dear Princess.

'I look so like the King, Rose, that I really don't think it would be a good idea for me to go to Ruritania,' I said. 'Surely you can see that?'

'I think you're just making excuses,' said Rose.

My brother looked at me curiously again. 'I can see that the man in your photograph isn't you, but the picture in the paper looks just like you.'

'Well I think I look more like the photograph,' I said, trying to sound relaxed, 'But I still won't go to Strelsau, Bob.'

'No, don't go to Strelsau, Rudolf,' he said. 'I don't think it would be a good idea at all.'

Since then, I have lived a very quiet life, though I often imagine myself in the crowded streets of Strelsau, or standing below the dark Castle of Zenda.

Once a year, I go to Dresden for a week, to meet my dear friend, Fritz von Tarlenheim. He tells me about what has been happening in Strelsau, about Sapt, the King, and often, of young Rupert. At last we speak about Flavia. Every year, Fritz brings me a box with a red rose in it. Round the rose is a piece of paper with the words, *Rudolf – Flavia – Always.* And I always send the same back to her with him.

That message and the rings we gave each other are all that now hold me and the Queen of Ruritania together. She has followed her duty to her country and married the King. There are times when I cannot bear to think of it. Other times, I thank God that I love the bravest and most wonderful lady in the world. Shall I see her again? I don't know. Somehow I think it's unlikely. But if I can never look at her sweet face again, or speak to her, then I must pray that, one day, my heart will find peace.

Reading Comprehension

1 **Choose the correct answer.**

1 Antoinette de Mauban decides to help Rudolf because...

A ☐ she doesn't want him to marry the Princess.

B ☐ she doesn't want him to be killed.

C ☐ she wants to leave Michael.

2 How does Fritz know where Rudolf is?

A ☐ He hears the girl scream.

B ☐ Antoinette and Johann tell him.

C ☐ He hears Rudolf shout at Rupert.

3 What does the young girl tell the Princess?

A ☐ The King is injured and is in the castle.

B ☐ The King is hiding behind some trees.

C ☐ She will show her the King, but only if she gives her money.

4 Why is Flavia worried?

A ☐ She thinks Rudolf has only pretended to love her.

B ☐ Now that she knows who Rudolf is, she no longer loves him.

C ☐ She knows that Rudolf cannot be trusted.

5 What explanation does George have for Rudolf's disappearance?

A ☐ He has been gossiping about Madame de Mauban.

B ☐ He has travelled to Paris to be with Madame de Mauban.

C ☐ He travelled to Strelsau to be with Madame de Mauban.

6 What does Flavia send Rudolf every year?

A ☐ Rudolf's dear friend, Fritz von Tarlenheim.

B ☐ A rose inside a box.

C ☐ A ticket to Dresden.

Vocabulary

2 How would you describe the characters below. Use any of the words from the box to help you. Add some words of your own to each column.

adventurous • brave • confident • dangerous • heroic • fearless
• passionate • romantic • sad • selfless • strong • trustworthy

Rudolf Rassendyll	Princess Flavia	Antoinette de Mauban

Writing

3 Imagine you are Rudolf Rassendyll at the end of the story. Write a letter to Flavia telling her about your journey home, your life in England, and what you remember most about your three months as King of Ruritania.

Speaking

4 Discuss the following statements.

1 *The Prisoner of Zenda* is one of the best adventure stories ever written.

2 The story is believable and fun.

3 The characters are interesting and realistic.

4 The love story between Rudolf Rassendyll and Princess Flavia is romantic.

Anthony Hope (1863–1933)

This late Victorian author is best known for his exciting adventure stories – *The Prisoner of Zenda*, and the second book in the series, *Rupert of Hentzau*. Hope was born in London in 1863, and he died in 1933, when he was 70 years old, at his house in Surrey. Anthony Hope's real name was Sir Anthony Hope Hawkins.

Early Years

Hope went to Marlborough School, and then studied law at Balliol College, Oxford. He became President of the Oxford Union – the famous student debating society.

After university, he went to the Inns of Court in London (where people train to become lawyers). Hope began work as a lawyer in 1887. At first, he loved the law, he said it gave him a chance to meet people from every part of society, but he also discovered that he loved writing!

A Difficult Decision

By 1892, Hope had published three novels, and was working on the next two, even though he was still working as a lawyer. These books did not make him much money, but, he wrote in his diary, that he had "received a lot of encouragement from the critics".

Hope began to find life difficult. Every hour that he was not working as a lawyer, he spent writing. At the end of 1892, he wrote in his diary "I almost hate having law now, it's come too late to please me, and it interrupts." Hope continued like this for two more "busy, but not very happy years", until one day...

"It was 28th November 1893 – I was walking back from the Westminster County Court (where I had won my case) when the idea of 'Ruritania' came into my head. I went back to my office, and thought about it, and the next day I wrote the first chapter."

The Prisoner of Zenda

Once he'd started writing *The Prisoner of Zenda,* Hope found he couldn't stop. He wrote every minute that he could, sometimes finishing two chapters a day. The work was going well until Hope found he had a problem. "I seemed to have got the Prisoner so tightly shut up in the Castle of Zenda," he says in his diary, "that it was impossible to get him out of it." It seems that both the writer and Rudolf Rassendyll found it difficult to rescue the King! Fortunately for us, Hope did solve his problem. He finished the novel in a month, and in April of 1894, *The Prisoner of Zenda* was published. The book was a great success with the public and the critics. This gave Hope the confidence, and the money, to leave the law to become a full-time writer.

The Celebrated Author

Hope was now quite famous, and there were often stories about him in the newspapers, which were not always true. Some of them he found quite funny.

"The journalist tells me that I leave my home at precisely 9.30 every morning, and walk along the Thames to Buckingham Street, sit down at my writing desk there as the clock strikes ten, write till it strikes one, go out to lunch, return at two, write till five, and... walk back again."

AMERICA

In 1897, Hope was invited to go to America to give public talks. The experience was enjoyable, and at least one American lady thought Hope was exactly like his hero Rassendyll!

LATER LIFE

Hope married Elizabeth Somerville in 1903. They had two sons and a daughter. During his life, Hope wrote 32 novels, and several plays, but today, he is only remembered for his adventures in Ruritania.

Task

1 What was Anthony Hope's real name?

_____

2 What two jobs did he have in his lifetime?

_____

3 What did he feel about being a lawyer while he was writing *The Prisoner of Zenda?*

_____

4 What made Hope become a full-time writer?

_____

Can I Buy a Ticket to Ruritania?

Ruritania is an invented country, but to many fans of the book it feels like a real place. Hope tells us that Ruritania is a small country just south of Dresden, probably somewhere in the German region of Bavaria.

Part of what makes Hope's invented country so real are the detailed descriptions of the landscape, the people and the customs of this tiny kingdom. Ruritania is a country of mountains, forests and medieval towns, but it's not cut off from the modern world. We know that the train runs directly from Dresden into Ruritania, and that the capital, Strelsau, has wide, modern streets.

The Politics of Ruritania

Where Ruritania is not modern, is in its politics. The country is not a democracy, but a place where the royal family has all the power. The army, led by Marshal Strakencz, is also under the control of the King. You could describe Ruritania as a police state! Rudolf tells us that he receives a report from the police every day. This tells him what everyone is doing, including his bad brother, Black Michael, and even includes a discussion on the private feelings of the Princess!

Task

1 Does Ruritania feel like a real place to you? Why?

2 Do you think that Ruritania is a good place to live? Why/why not?

3 Are you interested in news and gossip about the royal families of Europe? Why/why not?

A Revolution in Ruritania? Not Yet!

We know that while Ruritania has rich people, it also has a lot of poor people. Many of these work as servants. Although, there had been a lot of political change, and even some revolutions, in Europe during the nineteenth century, we can't imagine a revolution happening in Ruritania. The ordinary people seem more interested in the affairs of the royal family, than in working for a more equal society!

Syldavia

The Prisoner of Zenda was one of the first novels to make full use of an imagined country, but it was certainly not the last. We only have to think of Syldavia, the fictional country which Tintin visits in several of his adventures. The name for this country, which is "somewhere in the Balkans", was taken from Transylvania and Moldavia.

Like Ruritania, Syldavia has a royal family, and a small population. Tintin's creator, Hergé, gave Syldavia a capital city, Klow, a language, history, traditional cuisine, and a successful space programme.

Ruritania in Literature

Ruritania was inspired by a popular British view of central Europe during the nineteenth century. Many British people believed that this part of Europe was old fashioned, had forests filled with dangerous animals, and that the local people were rather primitive! In this stereotyped view, princes and kings were brave and handsome, and princesses were beautiful. Of course, there also had to be plenty of "baddies" trying to kill the king, and take power for themselves.

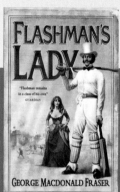

Flashman

George Macdonald Fraser, creator of the famous Flashman series, was inspired by Anthony Hope. *Royal Flash* is the second of the Flashman novels, and is based on the story of *The Prisoner of Zenda*. In it, Flashman has to pretend to be a Danish Prince who is about to marry a German Princess. The character of Flashman himself is the complete opposite of Rudolf Rassendyll. In Rudolf Rassendyll's position, he would certainly have killed the King, and kept the Princess and the crown for himself.

Task

1 Do you know of any other imaginary countries created by writers or film makers? _____

2 Who are your favourite heroes and villains? (They could come from a novel or a film.) _____

3 Why do you like them?_____

The Romantic Castles of Germany

Much of the action in this adventure story happens in castles and palaces. During the nineteenth century, many castles in Germany were rebuilt in a style that is called Castle Romanticism. At this time of relative peace, these castles were no longer needed for defence. They were built to impress visitors and to be beautiful. We can see this fashion in the chateau where Rudolf and his friends stay in Zenda, and in the new part of Michael's castle. These are described as modern and comfortable, with large windows.

The poor Prisoner of Zenda himself is not so fortunate. The castle where he is kept a prisoner is made from stone, it is medieval, and was not built for comfort. He is kept in an underground room, which must have been very damp, next to the moat.

Fairytales

Many people go to Germany to visit its fairy-tale castles. Any visit to these amazing buildings should include Hohenschwangau, which was built by Crown Prince Maximilian, Frederick the Great's Sanssouci palace outside Berlin, and Hohenzollern, built by the Prussian royal family.

Berg Eltz is perhaps everyone's idea of what a German castle should look like. It sits on top of a hill, has plenty of towers, and is surrounded by forests and a river.

Hohenschwangau

Neuschwanstein

One of the most famous castles dating from this time is Neuschwanstein Castle in southern Bavaria. It was built by Ludwig II, who was King of Bavaria until 1886. This stunning castle is built on top of a hill and, like Berg Eltz, is the perfect German castle. It is said to have been the inspiration for Sleeping Beauty's castle in Disneyland Park, California.

Neuschwanstein

Task

1 What are the main differences between the modern castles and the old castle we read about in this story?

_____

2 What is the link between King Ludwig II and Disneyland?

_____

Ludwig II – A Mysterious King

To this day, there is a mystery surrounding the story of King Ludwig II of Bavaria. He is known as the Swan King, and the Fairytale King, but he also became known as Mad King Ludwig.

Music and Architecture

Ludwig loved architecture. His most famous palaces at Neuschwanstein, Linderhof, and a replica of Versailles, called Herrenschiemsee Castle, are now visited by millions of people each year. Ludwig also loved music, and in particular the music of Wagner, who he supported financially for many years.

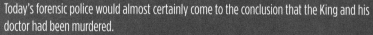

A Royal Murder?

When he was 41, Ludwig was told by his government that he was no longer fit to be a king. The public were informed that this was because he'd gone mad. Ludwig and his doctor were sent to Berg Castle, which Ludwig had used as his summer palace, and Ludwig's younger brother Otto was made king in his place.

The next morning, both Ludwig and his doctor were found dead in a shallow lake. Officially, their deaths were unexplained.

Berg Castle

Today's forensic police would almost certainly come to the conclusion that the King and his doctor had been murdered.

Although Ludwig's behaviour was strange, there is no good evidence that he was mad. After his death, Berg Castle became a museum. It has remained exactly as it was when Ludwig used to stay there.

Hope's Inspiration?

Hope wrote his story only a few years after these events. It is possible that Ludwig's tragic story provided inspiration for Hope's Rudolf of Ruritania. Rudolf, too, is described as mad and he has a younger brother. His doctor is held prisoner with him, though in the end, both Ludwig and his doctor are killed, while Prince Rudolf survives.

Task

1 What were some of Ludwig's favourite things? _____
2 What happened to King Ludwig? _____
3 Do you think he was murdered? Why? _____

The Prisoner of Zenda Goes to Hollywood

Only four years after Hope died, his book was made into a film. Released in 1937, it became an instant classic. The story of *The Prisoner of Zenda* was perfect material for the American film industry. There were princes and beautiful princesses, "goodies" and "baddies", and a fantastic adventure in a small, foreign country. Best of all, from a film maker's point of view, there were lots of sword fights.

When Rudolf Rassendyll, played by Ronald Colman, arrives in Ruritania on a fishing trip, he is surprised when everyone he meets stares at him. He thinks it's because he's English. He soon understands why they've been staring, when he meets the King of Ruritania.

In the film, Antoinette de Mauban plays a more active role than she does in the book. She is the one who comes up with the plan to rescue the King. By accident, she also helps Rupert to escape from Rassendyll and his friends. The sword fights are some of the most memorable scenes in the film. Douglas Fairbanks Jr. as Rupert Hentzau, and Raymond Massey as Duke Michael are both perfect villains!

Humour and Adventure

Humour is one of the things the film adaptations of the novel often miss. In the novel, the narrator, Rudolf Rassendyll, does not take himself too seriously. The reader is given plenty of opportunities to laugh at the characters and events. The gentle humour is one of the reasons that the novel is still so popular today. It's also a great story, and a great love story of course. For many people, *The Prisoner of Zenda* is one of the best adventure stories ever written.

Task

1 Do you like watching old movies? Why/why not?

2 Do you think film adaptations of books are usually better or worse than the original book? Can you give any examples?

Brothers of the Sword

When Rudolf meets his Ruritanian friends for the first time, Fritz immediately greets him as a "brother of the sword". In fact, the art and science of sword fighting was being replaced by guns by the end of the nineteenth century, but swords are a big part of Anthony Hope's story.

Sword fights make perfect cinema. In the 1937 film adaptation, Rudolf's fight with Rupert is particularly dramatic. If you look closely though, you will see that this is not a very realistic fight. In many films, the actors attack each other's swords rather than their bodies. Of course, in real life, the object is to kill or injure your enemy!

Sword facts

The word gladiator comes from the Latin word *gladius*, which means sword. Duels are formal fights between two men, and are almost always about 'honour'. Many famous people were involved in duels, including Miguel de Cervantes, Georg Friedrich Handel, and Aleksandr Pushkin.

Cinema's Best Sword Fights

The Duellists (1977) is Ridley Scott's first full-length film. It tells the story of two officers in Napoleon's army, D'Hubert, played by Keith Carradine, and Feraud, played by Harvey Keitel. These two men fight each other many times during their whole lives. This 'forgotten' classic has some of the most realistic sword fights in cinema.

The *Pirates of the Caribbean* series has some memorable sword fights. Though here, humour is more important than historical accuracy! While in *Star Wars,* swords are transformed into space-age light sabres in the dramatic final scene between Luke Skywalker and Darth Vader.

Task

1 What is a duel? _____
_____
2 Do you like seeing sword fights in films? _____
3 What do you think about fights in films? Do you like watching them or not? _____

TEST YOURSELF 自測

1 **Can you remember who said the following phrases from this story?**

1 'Rudolf Rassendyll, when are you going to do something?' (Ch.1)

2 'Well, aren't you lucky?' (Ch. 1)

3 'Come on Josef, let me have that cake.' (Ch. 2)

4 'The King? My God! The King?' (Ch. 2)

5 'They're coming! They're too soon!' (Ch.3)

6 'Tell my brother to kill me now. What's he waiting for?' (Ch.6)

7 'Black Michael will fall like the dog he is.' (Ch.6)

8 'Come on, man! Come and share the fun!' (Ch.8)

9 'He's dead! My God, the Duke's dead!' (Ch.8)

10 'Don't kiss him; he's not the King.' (Ch.9)

2 **Can you remember who...**

1 is waiting outside Flavia's private room in Chapter 3?_____
_____

2 is at the summerhouse? _____
_____

3 goes for a swim in the moat? _____
_____

4 gets killed in the King's prison room? _____
_____

5 George Featherly believes was the Prisoner of Zenda? _____
_____

3 **Can you draw a simple plan of Zenda, and the surrounding area? Try to include the town, 2 castles, forest and train station.**

SYLLABUS 語法重點和學習主題

Verbs
Present perfect continuous
Past perfect simple and
continuous
Future continuous
Future perfect
would for willingness/refusal
Third conditional
Wish, If only
Used to and would
Phrasal verbs
All passive forms
Contrast between continuous
and simple tenses
the Gerund

Conjunctions
Adverbs
More challenging adverbs
(building on base words e.g.
unpleasantly from pleasant)

Constructions with -ing
without, by, for, instead of

Determiners
either, neither, none, both
little, few, some,
enough, several, every, most

Sentence types
Relative clauses: embedded,
defining
Emphatic structures with *what*
Complex sentences, with a
variety of sub-clauses

Answer Key 答案

The Prisoner of Zenda

Pages 6-7
1a 1F; 2F; 3T; 4T; 5T; 6F
1b own answers
2 1 hero of the story; red hair and a big nose; 2 Rudolf's sister-in-law; 3 Rudolf's older brother, dark hair and eyes; 4 member of Rudolf's family, from the past, fell in love
3 1 Rose; 2 Rudolf; 3 Robert; 4 Rose; 5 Rudolf

Pages 16-17
1 1 Rose. She says he has done nothing with his life except enjoy himself. 2 Rudolf, he went to school and university in Germany. 3 Rudolf Elphberg will become Rudolf V of Ruritania in 3 weeks' time. 4 George Featherly, he works as a diplomat for the British Ambassador in Paris. 5 Antoinette de Mauban. 6 She is in love with the Duke of Strelsau, known as 'Black Michael'. He is the King's younger brother.
2 **Name**: Rudolf Rassendyll; **Age** 29; **Appearance**: red hair and large nose; **Languages and other skills**: fluent German, some French, Italian and Spanish, he is also good with a sword and can ride very well; **Hobbies**: he loves travelling; **Character**: is able to keep calm in a crisis
3 1 If I told him; 2 would have recognised; 3 had not left; 4 I would not have come here
4 own answers, students should check their answers after they have read this section in Chapter 2

Pages 26-27
1 1C; 2B; 3C; 4A; 5C; 6B
2 7, 2, 4, 8, 6, 3, 1, 5
3 loudly, unpleasantly, nervously, suspiciously, excitedly
4 1F; 2F; 3F; 4T; 5F; 6T

Pages 36-37
1 Any or all of the following points are possible.
> 2 the King's younger brother, is happy to send his men to kill Rudolf, is in a relationship with Antoinette de Mauban, but is in love with Princess Flavia, is also known as the Duke of Strelsau, would like to be king
> 3 loyal friend of the King, helps Rudolf, is an old soldier, is brave, usually finds a solution to difficult problems, is calm, intelligent and patient
> 4 beautiful, princess, cousin to Rudolf V and Black Michael, is pale, appears to be falling in love with Rudolf
> 5 English gentleman, brave, loyal, loves adventure, will risk his own life to help others, red hair, large nose, looks like the king of Ruritania, seems to be falling in love with Princess Flavia, has a good sense of humour, keeps his promises if he can
> 6 The Six are six men who work for Black Michael. De Gautet (French), Bersonin (Belgian), Detchard (English) and three Ruritanians, will not hesitate to use their guns
2 1 Sapt, Rudolf, Josef (dead); 2 The king; 3 Flavia, Rudolf, Black Michael; 4 Sapt; 5 Antoinette de Mauban, Rudolf; 6 Detchard, Bersonin, De Gautet; 7 Rudolf
3 1 open; 2 at; 3 like; 4 the; 5 into; 6 them; 7 down; 8 about; 9 on; 10 down; 11 but; 12 up
4 own answers
5 students practise use of dictionary, verbal phrases and listening for specific information

Pages 46-47

1a **1** Because the people are saying that she might marry Black Michael, and because the Princess herself is said to be unhappy that Rudolf has not visited her. **2** He wants him to ask the Princess to marry him. **3** That she has fallen in love with him. **4** Flavia tells Rudolf that she would show him all her love if he wasn't "king". **5** She interrupts him saying that she would consider him her king if he was a criminal and the Cardinal arrives. **6** If they wait more they will have problems **7** Flavia fears that going to hunt Michael could be dangerous for Rudolf. **8** He asks him to look after the Princess, kill Michael and make Flavia queen if he dies.

1b own answers

2 own answers (should include dancing, people looking at/talking about Rudolf and Flavia, Sapt interrupts Rudolf as he is about to reveal the truth, Rudolf and Flavia are shy with each other, they tell each other they are in love)

3 **1** impossible; **2** loveliest; **3** dishonest; **4** truth; **5** dangerous; **6** lier; **7** lovers; **8** worst

4 **1** rides a powerful horse; **2** wears fine clothes; **3** arrogant; **4** handsome; **5** young; **6** smiles a lot; **7** charming; **8** a bad person

Pages 56-57

1 **1**C; **2**B; **3**C; **4**A; **5**C; **6**A

2 own answers but students should include the old and new parts of the castle, the moat, the drawbridge, the stone steps leading down to the two rooms, the first room where the "six" stay, the king's prison, the window in his room and the large pipe that is blocking it, leading down into the moat

3 own answers, students should be encouraged to look back at what Johann says in this chapter

4 own answers

Pages 66-67

1 **1**F; **2**F; **3**T; **4**F; **5**T; **6**F; **7**F; **8**F; **9**T; **10**T; **11**T; **12**T

2 own answers, students should be encouraged to include the main events from Chapter 6, and, since this is a police report, to avoid putting in emotion, or conjecture, and concentrate on the facts

3a **1** had killed; **2** threw; **3** had killed; **4** rode; **5** had lost; **6** were; **7** were ; **8** had died; **9** were; **10** had managed

3b own answers (usually you use the past perfect to express something that has happened before what you express with the past simple—Reported speech)

4 own answers

5 **1**T; **2**F; **3**T; **4**T; **5**T; **6**F (at least Antoinette loves him!)

Pages 76-77

1a students should be encouraged to use their own words where possible. **1** To open the castle door at exactly two o'clock in the morning. **2** If all went well, then Sapt and his men would be at the door when Johann opened it. They were to rush in and attack the five servants. At the same moment, Madame de Mauban was to scream 'Help! Help! Michael help!' She would pretend that she was being attacked by Rupert. **3** At this point, Michael would come running out of his rooms, and there he would meet Sapt and his men. **4** Rupert would come across the bridge; De Gautet might or might not come with him. Rudolf would swim across the moat and hide under the drawbridge and then climb up onto it, and remove Rupert and De Gautet. **5** To go to the castle and demand to see the King. If the King was dead, then he must take Flavia immediately back to Strelsau, and make her queen. **6** He hid his horse and moved silently up to the castle. He tied a rope around himself, attached it to the tree, and lowered himself into the moat. He swam over to Jacob's Ladder. Then, he hid behind the great pipe and waited. **7** Rupert and De Gautet walked across the bridge and stopped in the middle. Rupert took a bottle from De Gautet, finished it, then threw it in the moat and started shooting at it. The first two shots missed but hit the pipe, the third hit the bottle. Then he fired several times at the pipe and Rudolf felt a bullet whistle past him. Then, a voice cried, 'Bridge closing!' and Rupert and De Gautet ran across. The bridge was raised. **8** Rupert came out of the old castle with a sword in his hand, climbed down some steps in the old wall, lowered himself into the water and swam across to the new part of the castle, with his sword between his teeth. When he reached the other side, he climbed up some other steps, unlocked a door, and disappeared. Rudolf swam over to the old side of the bridge and climbed halfway up the steps Rupert had just climbed down. Then he waited, sword in hand.

1b own answers, students should be encouraged to use the conditional tenses, and hypothetical constructions

2 1 b; **2** d; **3** a; **4** c

3 1 Antoinette; **2** Black Michael; **3** Black Michael; **4** Rupert; **5** Black Michael

Pages 86-87

1a **1** Rudolf waited; **2** key opening a door; **3** glass broken; **4** terrified woman; **5** Rudolf hid on the bridge; **6** door opened violently; **7** "Open the door!" **8** swords; **9** injured man; **10** Duke called out

1b students should be encouraged to use a variety of time connectives: next, then, at that point/moment, followed by etc. Possible answer:
Rudolf is waiting on the old side of the castle. It is quiet, then he hears a faint sound, like a key opening a door. Next, there is a crash from Madame de Mauban's room, to Rudolf it sounds as if something has been smashed. Immediately after that he hears a woman cry out and then she gives a terrified scream. Rudolf runs across the bridge and hides in total silence. Then there was another scream, followed by the sound of a door smashing against the wall. Rudolf hears Duke Michael shout "Open the door!", then a window opens above Rudolf's head in the old part of the castle and De Gautet shouts 'What's the matter?' Rudolf hears swords hitting each other and finally, the cry of someone who has been hurt.

2

Who...	gets killed (and by who)	gets injured (by who)	tries to kill Rupert
Antoinette de Mauban			x
Johann		x (Rupert)	
Black Michael	x (Rupert)		
De Gautet	x (Rudolf)		
Bersonin	x (Rudolf)		
the doctor	x (Detchard)		
Rudolf		x (Detchard)	x
Detchard	x (Rudolf)		
the King		x (Detchard)	
Rupert Hentzau		x (Rudolf)	
Fritz			x

3a,b own answers

4 1F; **2**F; **3**F; **4**F; **5**T; **6**F

Pages 98-99

1 1B; **2**C; **3**B; **4**A; **5**C; **6**B

2 own answers

3 own answers (students should try to respect the style of the story and its setting)

4 own answers

Page 101

1 Sir Anthony Hope Hawkins;

2 lawyer, writer;

3 He almost started to hate being a laywer because it inerrupted his work as writer;

4 *The Prisoner of Zenda* was a great success with the public and the critics and this gave him the confidence and money to leave the law and become a full-time writer.

Page 102-103

own answers

Page 104

1 possible answer:
The old castles were places where kings and queens usually lived, with all the necessary for a battle or worse a plague. Modern castles are only tourist attractions for visitors.

2 King Ludwig II's castle is said to be the inspiration for Sleeping Beauty's castle in Disneyland, California.

Page 105

1 own answers

2 Architecture and music. He seemed to have become mad and for this he couldn't be a king any more ; soon he was found dead in a shallow lake.

3 own answers

Page 106

1-2 own answers

Page 107

1 It's a fight between two or more people who use swords or other arms.

2-3 own answers

Page 109

1 **1** Rose Rassendyll; **2** George Featherly; **3** The King; **4** Sapt; **5** Antoinette de Mauban; **6** The King; **7** Rupert Hentzau; **8** Rudolf Rassendyll; **9** Antoinette de Mauban; **10** Sapt

2 **1** Fritz, De Gautet, Bersonin and Detchard; **2** Rudolf, Antoinette de Mauban, and three of the "Six" De Gautet, Bersonin and Detchard; **3** Rudolf and Rupert; **4** the doctor and Detchard; **5** Antoinette de Mauban

3 own answer

Read for Pleasure: *The Prisoner of Zenda* 古堡藏龍

作　　者：Anthony Hope
改　　寫：Elizabeth Ferretti
繪　　畫：Barbara Baldi Bargiggia
照　　片：Shutterstock, ELI Archive
責任編輯：傅薇
封面設計：涂慧
出　　版：商務印書館（香港）有限公司
　　　　　香港筲箕灣耀興道 3 號東滙廣場 8 樓
　　　　　http://www.commercialpress.com.hk
發　　行：香港聯合書刊物流有限公司
　　　　　香港新界大埔汀麗路 36 號中華商務印刷大廈 3 字樓
印　　刷：中華商務彩色印刷有限公司
　　　　　香港新界大埔汀麗路 36 號中華商務印刷大廈 14 字樓
版　　次：2016年9月第 1 版第 1 次印刷
　　　　　© 2016 商務印書館（香港）有限公司
　　　　　ISBN 978 962 07 0483 3
　　　　　Printed in Hong Kong
　　　　　版權所有　不得翻印

Read for Pleasure 系列為高小至初中英語學習者提供英文讀本，包括經典名著和現代故事，分 Basic、Intermediate 和 Advanced 三級。內容豐富，設計具現代感，在享受閱讀之樂的同時，可提升聽說讀寫的能力。

年輕的英國紳士魯德夫遊歷中歐小國時，竟發現自己和國王長得一模一樣。魯德夫為失蹤的國王擔當替身，卻愛上將與國王訂婚的美麗公主。他能否成功拯救國王？會否為了迎娶公主而放棄救人？

Level	Number of Headwords	Cambridge Examinations
Basic	600 – 800 headwords	Movers Flyers/Key (KET)
Intermediate	1000 – 1600 headwords	Preliminary (PET)
Advanced	1800 – 2500 headwords	First (FCE) Advanced (CAE)

代理商 聯合出版
電話 02-25868596
NT: 310.

陳列類別：英語學習　　HK$ 68.00

網上商店

超閱網
SuperBookcity.com

聯合出版集團

ISBN 978 962 07 0483 3
9 789620 704833

商務印書館（香港）有限公司
http://www.commercialpress.com.hk
PUBLISHED AND PRINTED IN HONG KONG